A PENGUIN MYSTERY

AUNT DIMITY'S DEATH

Nancy Atherton is also the author of *Aunt
Dimity and the Duke, Aunt Dimity's Good Deed,
Aunt Dimity Digs In, Aunt Dimity's Chirstmas,* and
Aunt Dimity Beats the Devil. She recently moved
out of the cornfields but still resides in central
Illinois, where she is working on her next book
in the Aunt Dimity series.

Aunt Dimity's Christmas

Nancy Atherton

PENGUIN BOOKS

PENGUIN BOOKS
Published by the Penguin Group
Penguin Putnam Inc., 375 Hudson Street,
New York, New York 10014, U.S.A.
Penguin Books Ltd, 27 Wrights Lane, London W8 5TZ, England
Penguin Books Australia Ltd, Ringwood, Victoria, Australia
Penguin Books Canada Ltd, 10 Alcorn Avenue,
Toronto, Ontario, Canada M4V 3B2
Penguin Books (N.Z.) Ltd, 182–190 Wairau Road,
Auckland 10, New Zealand

Penguin Books Ltd, Registered Offices:
Harmondsworth, Middlesex, England

First published in the United States of America by Viking Penguin,
a member of Penguin Putnam Inc. 1999
Published in Penguin Books 2000

5   7   9   10   8   6   4

PUBLISHER'S NOTE
This is a work of fiction. Names, characters, places, and incidents are
either the product of the author's imagination or are used fictitiously,
and any resemblance to actual persons, living or dead, business
establishments, events, or locales is entirely coincidental.

THE LIBRARY OF CONGRESS HAS CATALOGED
THE HARDCOVER EDITION AS FOLLOWS:
Atherton, Nancy.
Aunt Dimity's Christmas/Nancy Atherton.
p.   cm.
ISBN 0-670-88453-7 (hc.)
ISBN 0 14 02.9630 1 (pbk.)
I. Title.
PS3551.T426A935   1999
813'.54—dc21   99–36750

Printed in the United States of America
Set in Perpetua
Designed by Patrice Sheridan

FOR
MOM AND DAD,
MY HEROES

My father died when I was three months old. I don't recall his laughter or his touch. My memories of him came secondhand, through my mother's words and well-thumbed photo albums.

"Your father was a soldier," my mom told me, and there he is, in grainy black-and-white, with his GI grin and rumpled uniform, standing in the ruins of Berlin. Kids in ragged clothing cluster near him, holding high the gifts he's taken from a tattered duffel bag—chocolate bars and chewing gum, socks and stocking caps, bits and bobs finagled from his squad. No department-store Santa ever looked half so merry as my dad did that day, among the children in the ruins of Berlin.

"Your father's favorite holiday was Christmas," my mother said, and fully half the photos in the albums prove her point. There he is, years later, playing Santa at our church on the west side of Chicago, baking angel cookies to give to friends and neighbors, placing the star atop one glittering tree after another. While my father was alive,

Christmas began on my mother's birthday, the fourteenth of December, and climaxed with a lavish party on Christmas Eve.

Christmas Day was spent recuperating.

After my father's death, my mother cut back on the festivities, for emotional as well as financial reasons. When I was growing up, there was always a whiff of mourning in the crisp winter air. No one had to tell me not to compare my father's extravagant celebrations with my mother's humbler holidays, but I secretly lived for the day when my Christmases would match those in the photographs.

"The day has finally come," I murmured. I curled my legs beneath me on the cushioned window seat and gazed upward at the sky. I was a grown woman now, with two children of my own, and the lean times I'd endured after my mother's death were a thing of the past. Thanks to an unexpected inheritance from a family friend, I possessed a cottage in England and a fortune large enough to celebrate Christmas as lavishly as I pleased. This year, I vowed, my father's favorite holiday would again be a time of jubilation, freed at last from any hint of sorrow.

The crescent moon sailed serenely between lowering clouds, and the dead leaves on the beech hedge fluttered dryly in a bitter northeast wind. I eyed the heavy-laden clouds intently and shivered with anticipation. Christmas— my first Christmas in England and my sons' first Christmas ever—was a mere two weeks away. I wanted it to be perfect.

It was unfortunate, to be sure, that my nanny had temporarily abandoned her post to enjoy a prolonged holiday in Italy with her fiancé. The twins were nine months old and fearfully mobile. It was no easy task to keep them from killing themselves and/or dismantling the cottage, but my father-in-law accepted the challenge without a second thought.

William Willis, Sr., arrived at the cottage the day after my nanny departed, and insisted on assuming her duties. Willis, Sr., was no fair-weather grandfather. He was a fastidious, patrician gentleman in his mid-sixties, a Boston Brahmin and a lawyer of high repute, but his passion for fine tailoring was nothing compared to his passion for his grandsons.

He slept on a rollaway bed in the nursery, got the boys up in the morning, read stories to them at night, and took dirty diapers, flying farina, and splashy baths in stride. When I commented wonderingly on his devotion, he informed me that since he'd never expected to live long enough to see his son's sons, he intended to make every moment with them count.

With Willis, Sr., in residence, I was able to go full speed ahead with my holiday plans. I took stock of my winter wardrobe and declared it null and void. My blue jeans and Salvation Army sweaters reminded me too strongly of the bad old days, so I dispatched the lot to Oxfam and filled my closet with silk-lined, custom-tailored trousers and tops that ran the gamut from raw silk to handspun wool to jewel-toned velvets. I replaced my ratty sneakers with handmade Italian boots, in suede and buttery leather, and my even rattier bathrobe with a vintage 1940s dressing gown in the softest shades of gray and baby blue. I splurged on a sumptuous black cashmere swing coat with a shawl collar I could snug around my face when the harsh winds blew. I'd never been a clotheshorse, but I was learning fast.

Once I'd refreshed my wardrobe, I escorted my husband to Oxford to be fitted for a Father Christmas suit. While he was at the tailor's, I hunted down exquisite antique ornaments and a lacy spun-glass star for the top of the tree. Bill and I plundered London on a dozen shopping sprees, buying gifts for everyone we knew.

We roamed the bridle path in the oak grove near the cottage, harvesting evergreen boughs, bunches of holly, and sprigs of mistletoe, and brought home a living Christmas tree from a nursery near Oxford. I invited Bill's English relatives to our Christmas Eve bash and arranged for them to spend the night at Anscombe Manor, the spacious home belonging to my closest friend and nearest neighbor, Emma Harris. I ordered a goose, a turkey, and two hams for the party, along with sundry accompaniments, and stockpiled ingredients for the daily round of baking that would fill the cottage with holiday aromas.

The decorating, the baking, the wrapping of presents, and the warbling of carols would begin tomorrow, the fourteenth of December, my late mother's birthday. I could hardly wait.

Even now, I could picture the living room, the hallway, the staircase, the entire cottage lit with candles, wreathed with evergreen garlands, and decked with boughs of holly. Best of all, I could envision my family—husband, father-in-law, and sons—gathered before the hearth, with mugs of hot cocoa and plates of angel cookies, enjoying the special peace of Christmastime.

There was only one thing missing from my perfect celebration. I leaned forward to breathe upon the window-pane and wrote with a fingertip in the frosty condensation: *snow.* I wanted snow so badly I could taste it. I wanted it to fall in drifts and block the lanes and transform the furrowed fields into something pristine and magical. I longed to watch my sons' eyes widen as the cottage disappeared beneath a sparkling cascade of swirling flakes. When the heavy clouds swallowed the slender moon, I peered upward and rejoiced.

My husband cleared his throat and I turned to face the living room. Bill sat in his favorite armchair, clad in a crewneck sweater and twill trousers, gazing pensively into the middle distance. Willis, Sr., dressed down for the evening in creased pajamas, leather slippers, and a magnificent paisley dressing gown, sat in an armchair on the opposite side of the hearth, reading a novel. A fire, lit after the babies were safely tucked up in the nursery, crackled merrily and cast a rosy glow over the low-ceilinged, comfortably furnished room.

I sighed with pleasure and gazed adoringly at Bill. He would make a splendid Father Christmas. If anyone had been born to play the role of a gift-giving saint, it was my gentle, great-hearted husband.

Bill cleared his throat once more and folded his hands over his stomach. "Christmas," he stated flatly, "should be abolished."

"Huh?" I said, startled.

"Christmas should be abolished," said Bill, biting off each word. "I'm sick to death of it."

"But it hasn't even started yet," I objected.

Bill blinked rapidly. "It hasn't started? Then what have we been doing for the past month?"

"Getting warmed up," I replied.

"Lori," Bill said slowly, "do you realize that we've been to fifteen parties in the past ten days?"

"Has it been that many?" I said. "I guess I wasn't counting."

Bill's laughter held a touch of madness. "Seven dinner parties, five luncheons, and three sherry evenings, in addition to running back and forth from London every other

day, not to mention all the little jaunts to Oxford, on top
of playing woodsman in the oak grove . . . Lori," he
gasped, "I'm worn out."

"Of course you are." I crossed quickly to sit on the arm
of Bill's chair, smoothed the hair back from his forehead,
and cooed, "It was thoughtless of me to pile so much on
you, but you know how hard it is to refuse an invitation
without offending someone. I'll go to the rest of the parties by myself, okay? All you have to do between now and
Christmas Eve is bring the tree in from the garden shed
tomorrow."

Bill leaned his head against the back of the chair and
breathed a sigh of relief. "I think I can manage that."

I smiled sweetly. "And play Joseph in the Nativity play."

Bill's eyes swiveled toward my face. "Nativity play?"

I got to my feet and put a couple of yards between me
and my great-hearted husband before asking, "Didn't I tell
you about the Nativity play?"

"No," Bill said, with frightening calm, "you didn't."

"Well," I said, taking a deep breath, "Peggy Kitchen decided to stage a Nativity play on Christmas Eve, but according to her, Nativity plays are always directed by the
vicar's wife, so she corralled Lilian Bunting into directing
it, only Lilian's never directed a play before, and there was
a shortage of male volunteers for the cast, so I"—I backed
up another step—"I volunteered you."

Bill lowered his chin in the manner of a bull about to
charge. "You'll have to unvolunteer me, Lori."

"It's mainly tableaux," I coaxed. "Hardly any lines to
memorize. And they're only holding four rehearsals."

"No," said Bill.

"Not even as a favor to Lilian?" I pleaded.

"No," Bill repeated.

"Bill," I said sternly, "it's your civic duty to help the vicar's wife."

"Civic duty?" Bill sputtered, pushing himself up from his chair. "You've had civic duty on the brain ever since the Harvest Festival last summer. Well, here's a news flash for you, Lori: I danced with the morris dancers at the festival, I singed my eyebrows lighting the Guy Fawkes Day bonfire, and I bought a year's worth of beeswax candles for Saint George's Church at the last benefit auction. I've *done* my civic duty, and I plan to spend the next two weeks *at home*."

Red-faced with fury, Father Christmas stormed out of the living room, slammed open the stair gate, slammed it shut behind him, and stomped up to the master bedroom. I stood frozen in place until his last foot-thump faded, then leaned against the mantelpiece and groaned.

Willis, Sr., looked up from his novel. "My son is tired," he offered.

"Your son is right." I sank into the chair Bill had vacated. "I never should have accepted all of those invitations."

"Christmas comes but once a year," said Willis, Sr. "It is only natural to wish to share the joys of the season with friends."

"Maybe," I said, refusing consolation, "but I definitely could have planned our trips better. If I'd arranged things properly, we wouldn't have had to run back and forth to London and Oxford so often."

"My son is accustomed to letting employees run for him," Willis, Sr., observed. "I do not think it such a bad thing for him to do his own running now and again."

"Okay," I allowed, "but I shouldn't have volunteered him for the Nativity play without speaking with him first."

"No," Willis, Sr., agreed, "you should not have."

I folded my arms and slumped back. "Now Bill's mad at me and I've left Lilian in the lurch."

"I can do little to remedy the former predicament," said Willis, Sr., "but I may be able to help with the latter." He ran a finger along his immaculately shaved jaw. "Perhaps I could take Bill's place in the Nativity play."

I shot upright in my chair. "Are you serious?"

"I do not pretend to be a polished thespian," Willis, Sr., cautioned, "but I believe I could fulfill the role of Joseph without embarrassing myself or Mrs. Bunting."

"Lilian will weep with gratitude," I assured him.

"Then you may tell her not to worry about finding another Joseph," said Willis, Sr., with a decisive nod. He picked up his novel. "And now I believe you have some diplomatic business to conduct upstairs?"

I beamed at him. "What would I do without you, William?"

"I tremble to think," he replied.

I gave him a peck on the cheek, then headed for the staircase, hoping that Bill had been too angry to fall asleep at once. When I reached the head of the stairs, I turned automatically toward the nursery to check on the twins and saw, in the night-light's dim glow, that Bill had beaten me to the punch.

I watched in silence as my husband bent low to place a handsome pink flannel rabbit at the foot of Rob's crib. When he straightened, I whispered, "I'm sorry."

"You should be," Bill whispered back, but he put a hand out to me, to take the sting from his words.

"Don't worry about a thing," I told him, taking his hand in mine. "From now on, we're having a quiet Christmas at home. Except for the Christmas Eve party."

"I should be recovered by then." Bill pulled me close and wrapped his arms around me. A few moments later he murmured softly in my ear, "Your willingness to make amends shall be rewarded, my love."

"How?" I asked huskily, running my fingers through his hair.

"With snow," he replied.

My hands dropped to his shoulders. It was not the answer I'd expected.

Bill drew me to the window. "I don't know if it'll last until Christmas, but it's a start."

A shimmering veil of snow swirled and billowed just beyond the windowpane. Fat flakes, wind-driven, splashed the glass or cartwheeled through the darkness to deepen drifts already forming along the flagstone path. It was dazzling, hypnotic, an answer to my prayers—I would have stood there all night, entranced, if my husband hadn't suggested a better way to spend the evening.

Hours later, long after Bill and I had fallen asleep, after Willis, Sr., had closed his book, quenched the fire, and crept upstairs to bed, the snow kept falling. It curled like ermine along bare boughs, filled furrows in plowed fields, and drifted gently over the tattered stranger sprawled beside my graveled drive.

The gift the stranger carried nearly cost him his life.

A soft knock at the bedroom door awoke me the following morning. I lay for a moment, relishing the warmth of Bill's body, then slipped out of bed and pulled on the vintage dressing gown I'd picked up in London. I paused briefly to admire the robe's pastel gray-and-blue plaid before tiptoeing barefoot into the hall.

My father-in-law awaited me, fully dressed and sincerely apologetic. "I am sorry to disturb you, Lori, but my grandsons are rather excitable this morning and I cannot find a way to calm them." He hesitated. "Have you any idea what 'wedge' means?"

"Wedge?" I echoed blankly.

Willis, Sr., nodded. "Rob and Will keep repeating it, 'wedge, wedge, wedge,' as if it had a particular meaning."

I felt the hairs on the back of my neck prickle. Until now the twins' intelligible vocabulary had consisted of a handful of generic terms, such as "mama" and "dada," and the highly original "gaga," meaning—one hoped—

grandfather. Had my little geniuses added a proper noun
to their lexicon?

"Where are they?" I asked.

"In the nursery," Willis, Sr., replied, leading the way
down the hall. "I closed the door, fearing that you and Bill
might be awakened by the commotion."

As Willis, Sr., opened the nursery door, I heard a babble
of baby voices loud enough to wake the dead. Will and
Rob, still dressed in their pajamas, their dark hair tousled
and their cheeks pink with excitement, were standing in
their cribs, bouncing up and down and chattering wildly.

"You see?" said Willis, Sr.

"Mama," cried Will. "Wedge, wedge, wedge."

"Wedge!" added Rob, in case I'd missed the point.

"What's going on?" Bill appeared in the doorway, rub-
bing sleep from his eyes, wearing a hastily donned Harvard
sweatshirt and gray sweatpants.

"I think they're trying to tell us something," I murmured, scanning the room.

"Spoken like a doting mother," Bill said, with a tolerant
smile. "You know the boys are too young to—"

I nudged him with my elbow and pointed toward the
window seat. "Wedge," I said triumphantly.

If Bill had remembered to put on his glasses, he'd've
cracked the code as quickly as I had. It didn't take a genius
to figure out that "wedge" meant Reginald, the pink flannel rabbit bestowed upon me at birth by Aunt Dimity.

"What's Reginald doing on the window seat?" Bill
pulled his glasses from the pocket of his sweatshirt and put
them on. "I dropped him in Rob's crib last night."

"Rob must have tossed him out," I said.

"All the way to the window seat?" Bill frowned. "That's
a heck of a toss for a little guy. Besides, Reginald's standing

upright, facing the window. How did he land like that? Father, did you—"

"I did not move Reginald," said Willis, Sr., crossing to look out of the window. "He was sitting on the window seat when I awoke this morning. I thought one of you had placed him there."

A quiver of uneasiness passed through me. The boys had fallen silent and were watching me expectantly. I nodded to them and joined Willis, Sr., at the window, squinting against the glare of bright sunlight on snow.

Not a whisper of wind stirred the silent world beyond the windowpane. The sky was a cloudless dome of blue, and the drab autumnal landscape was now gowned in classic white. The hedgerows sported clusters of sparkling pompoms, and the front lawn wore a sinuous, shimmering gown that flowed unbroken from the flagstone walk to the foot of the lilac bushes lining the graveled drive.

"What's that?" Bill asked, coming up behind me.

"What's what?" I replied.

Willis, Sr., leaned forward. "I believe I see something beneath the lilac bushes."

Bill stiffened suddenly. "Something . . . or someone."

For half a heartbeat, no one moved. Then Reginald tumbled from the window seat to the floor, stirring all of us into action. Willis, Sr., remained with the boys while Bill and I pelted down the stairs, leaving the gates open in our haste. We paused briefly at the front door to jam our bare feet into boots, then raced outside, not bothering with jackets.

A man lay on his side beneath the bare-branched lilac bushes, his arms crossed over his chest and his knees half-bent, as though conserving a last remnant of body heat. Shoulder-length gray hair fell across his face, and his shaggy beard was rimed with frost. The man was dressed

like a tramp, in ragged trousers, fingerless gloves, and a
worn woolen overcoat bound at the waist with a length of
rope. A drift of snow had settled over him, intricately pat-
terned with whorls and curves.

Bill dropped to his knees and pressed his fingers to the
man's neck. "Still with us," he muttered. "Just barely. Grab
his legs, Lori."

I looked at the man's ragged trousers, suppressed a
shudder of revulsion, then reached for his legs and lifted.

Willis, Sr., was slight of build and had a delicate consti-
tution, but when he took charge in an emergency he had
the command capability of a five-star general. While Bill
and I were out in the snow, he got on the telephone.

In less than an hour, an RAF rescue helicopter appeared
in my back meadow and whisked the tramp off to the
Radcliffe Infirmary in Oxford, where he was treated by a
team of specialists—commandeered by my well-connected
father-in-law—for pneumonia complicated by hypother-
mia and malnutrition.

Dr. Pritchard, the attending physician, kept us informed
of his patient's progress throughout the morning. At nine-
fifteen the doctor reported that the man was in critical
condition, still unconscious and still without a name. The
police had been unable to identify him, and the medical
staff had found no trace of identification on his person.

We maintained a silent vigil in the living room. Willis,
Sr., stood with his hands clasped behind his back, staring
out of the bow windows toward the lilac bushes, while Bill
and I sat in armchairs, facing each other across the cold
hearth.

The twins had gone through their morning routine with
unaccustomed docility, as though sensing the gravity of

the situation. Rob had spent the past half hour in Bill's lap, chewing diligently on Reginald's left ear, while Will curled contentedly in my arms.

The sofa, where we'd placed the tramp, was still damp from a drizzle of snowmelt. I would have to have it cleaned, I thought, and spray it with disinfectant before I let my sons anywhere near it.

"I wonder what he was doing here," Bill mused aloud.

"What difference does it make?" I asked. "He's in good hands. We don't have to worry about him anymore."

"But don't you think it's strange that he should come here?" Bill went on. "We're not on a main thoroughfare." Aunt Dimity's cottage was, in fact, tucked away on a narrow lane that scarcely merited a mention on most road maps.

"Perhaps he was hitchhiking," Willis, Sr., proposed, "and the driver dropped him short of his destination."

"I doubt it," said Bill. "Only locals use our lane, and none of our neighbors would dump a sick man in a snowdrift."

Willis, Sr., pursed his lips. "Are you suggesting that the gentleman came here intentionally, to see one of you?"

"That's ridiculous," I said. "Bill and I don't know any derelicts."

"That's true," said Bill, "but he might have come here to see——" He broke off and cocked an ear toward the window. "Does anyone else hear bells?"

A smile wreathed Willis, Sr.'s face as he leaned forward to peer out of the bay window. "I believe Lady Eleanor has come to call."

Lady Eleanor, commonly known as Nell Harris, lived up the road in a fourteenth-century manor house with her father and stepmother, Derek and Emma Harris. Nell was thirteen years old, tall, willowy, brilliant, and ethereally beautiful. She frightened the life out of most adults, but Willis, Sr., thought she walked on water.

I carried Will to the window to watch Nell arrive with her usual panache, emerging from the bridle path in a one-horse open sleigh, with two passengers in the backseat and Bertie, her chocolate-brown teddy bear, by her side.

Nell's passengers were immediately recognizable because they were a matched set. Ruth and Louise Pym were identical twin sisters old enough to remember the boys marching off to the blood-soaked fields of Flanders. They were astonishingly spry, a tiny bit vague, and always identically dressed.

Today they looked as though they'd stepped out of a Currier and Ives print. They wore high-waisted coats of fine black wool with puffed shoulders trimmed in black braid. Their dainty hands were protected by white rabbit muffs, their heads by feathered bonnets, and their shoes, incongruously, by ungainly rubber boots.

While Nell stabled her horse in the shed her father had built at the end of the bridle path, the Pyms fluttered up the snow-covered flagstone walk. I handed Will to his grandfather and hastened to the front door to welcome them.

"We're sorry to be so long in coming," Ruth began, as I ushered them into the hallway. "Dear sweet Nell was kind enough to transport us . . ."

". . . in her sleigh," Louise continued. The Pyms' alternating speech pattern was as distinctive as their antiquated clothing. "Our motor, as you know, requires a great deal of coaxing . . ."

". . . to start in such weather," Ruth went on. Since the Pyms' "motor" had been built shortly after the horse-and-buggy era, it was a miracle that it started in any weather.

"Otherwise, we would have been here much sooner. Except that the snow might have . . ."

". . . impeded our progress," explained Louise. "The lane is blocked from here to Finch, and Mr. Barlow hasn't yet plowed."

I felt a familiar sense of confusion settle over me as I took their coats and helped them step out of their boots. I had no idea why the Pyms were apologizing for their late arrival, since I'd never expected them in the first place.

"Did we have plans for this morning?" I asked.

"We certainly did," said Ruth. "Louise and I are woefully behind in our crochet work, and unless we get started soon . . ."

". . . we shall not be able to deliver our Christmas presents on time," said Louise worriedly. "However, such plans are of no consequence when compared with the urgent business at hand."

"Right," I said, knowing that all would be made clear eventually. "Please, come in. Bill? Will you see to our guests?"

While my husband looked after the Pyms, I went to the kitchen to put the kettle on. I'd just carried the tea tray into the living room when Nell knocked at the front door. I placed the tray on the coffee table and hastened to let her in.

Nell Harris swept into the cottage with Bertie in the crook of her arm. Bertie looked like a fuzzy elf in his forest-green sweater and red-and-green-striped scarf, but Nell looked like a snow queen. Her hooded velvet cloak was nearly as blue as her eyes, and her golden curls gleamed like a crown in the bright morning light.

"Please, tell us he isn't dead," she said, her voice quivering with emotion.

"Who?" I asked.

"Reginald," she replied, as if the answer were self-evident. "Bertie's been frantic ever since he saw the rescue helicopter flying toward the cottage. Has an accident be-fallen Reginald?"

Nell's myriad eccentricities had long since ceased to amaze me. If she wanted to believe that her teddy bear was worried sick about my pink flannel rabbit, who was I to criticize? I was simply thankful that she hadn't dyed her golden hair black or defiled her fair skin with tattoos.

"Reginald's fine," I said, taking her cape, "apart from a little baby drool in the ear."

"Thank heavens," Nell said fervently. She paused, then asked in a puzzled voice, "Are Ruth and Louise right, then? Did you really call out the RAF to rescue a tramp?"

I stared at her. "How did Ruth and Louise know about him?"

Nell shrugged. "I have no idea. They flagged me down as I was riding past their house and asked me to take them here directly, because they were worried about a tramp. Did you really call out the RAF—"

"Yes, Nell," I said. "In fact, William called out the RAF to rescue a tramp. Is that so hard to believe?"

Nell's blue eyes became thoughtful. "I suppose not. I've just never heard of anyone doing it before."

"Come on," I said. "I want to find out what the Pyms know about my uninvited guest."

Nell exchanged greetings with Bill and Willis, Sr., and bestowed a kiss apiece on Rob and Will, neatly dodging Will's attempts to grab a handful of enticing golden curls. She coaxed Rob into trading Reginald for a purple plush dinosaur and placed my pink rabbit on the window seat with Bertie before perching on an ottoman beside Willis, Sr.'s chair.

I sat on the couch, bracketed by the Pyms, and began to

serve the tea, wondering how long it would take the loquacious sisters to come to the point of their visit. They surprised me by coming to it at once.

"We knew the moment we heard the helicopter that something terrible had happened," said Ruth. "Such a pity. If only the poor gentleman . . ."

". . . had come into our house, as we asked him to." Louise shook her head sadly. "But he wouldn't stop."

I looked from one sister to the other. "Did you speak with the tramp last night?"

"We heard him coughing on the bridle path," Ruth replied, "a terrible, racking cough. Louise called to him, and I offered him hot soup . . ."

". . . but he wouldn't stop." Louise's bright bird's eyes widened as she added, "It was rather eerie, to be honest. He reminded us so strongly . . ."

". . . of poor Robert Anscombe, who died so long ago," said Ruth. "He lost an arm in the trenches in 1917, and his face was so sadly disfigured that he couldn't bear to be with other people . . ."

". . . so he always took the bridle path, to avoid being seen," Louise finished.

I saw Nell nod. The Harrises had lived in Anscombe Manor for the past eight years. The house had been a wreck when they'd moved into it, and the grounds had been sorely neglected. The Anscombe family, once Finch's local gentry, had faded from the scene some thirty years earlier. Now there was little to remember them by but a pair of effigies and assorted marble plaques in Saint George's Church.

"We urged him to come in out of the storm," said Ruth, "but he said he would be stopping soon enough."

"Where?" said Bill.

"At Dimity Westwood's cottage," said Louise.

Of course, I thought. If the tramp had come to the cottage to see anyone, it had to have been Dimity Westwood. The woman from whom I'd inherited the cottage had known a wide range of people during her lifetime, including those at the lowest end of the social scale.

Willis, Sr., shifted Will from his shoulder to his lap before stating the obvious. "The gentleman must be ignorant of the fact that Miss Westwood is dead."

The sisters nodded in tandem.

"We tried to tell him," Ruth said. "But he couldn't hear us . . ."

". . . over the wind," said Louise, "and the coughing."

"Did he say anything else about Dimity?" Bill asked.

"Nothing," said Ruth. "He simply waved . . ."

". . . and went on his way," said Louise. "We've been terribly concerned about him. How is the poor gentleman?"

Bill caught my eye and jutted his chin toward the hallway. While he launched into a detailed description of the morning's activities, I excused myself and headed for the study. It was clear that my husband wanted me to speak with Aunt Dimity.

3

Dimity Westwood was not, in an official sense, my aunt. Nor was she, technically speaking, alive. The former was far easier to explain than the latter.

Dimity Westwood had been my late mother's closest friend. They'd met in London during the Second World War and maintained a steady correspondence long after the war was over. I grew up hearing about Aunt Dimity, but only as a fictional character in a series of bedtime stories. I didn't learn about the real Dimity Westwood until after her death, when she bequeathed to me a considerable fortune, a honey-colored cottage in the Cotswolds, and a blue leather–bound journal with blank pages, which I kept on a shelf in the study.

It was through the blue journal that I came to know my benefactress. Dimity Westwood was not the sort of person who'd let a little thing like death interrupt the habits of a lifetime, so she continued her correspondence long after her mortal remains had dwindled into dust.

When I opened the blue journal, Aunt Dimity's handwriting appeared, an elegant copperplate taught in the village school at a time when high-buttoned shoes were still in vogue. I had no idea how Dimity managed to bridge the gap between earth and eternity, and I kept the blue journal a closely held secret, but I cherished her presence in the cottage and hoped she would never leave.

"Dimity?" I sat in one of the pair of tall leather armchairs that flanked the hearth, with the journal open in my lap. I glanced at the closed door and kept my voice low, understandably reluctant to have my guests hear me addressing a dead woman. "Dimity?" I repeated, and felt a thrill course though me as the familiar, gracefully curving lines of royal-blue ink began to loop and curl across the page.

Good morning, my dear, and what a beautiful morning it is. You must be so very pleased. The snow came, just as you hoped it would.

"Let's not talk about snow right now," I said shortly. "We have something else to discuss."

And what might that be?

"An old guy nearly froze to death in the drive last night," I said.

How dreadful.

"Apparently, he was coming here to see you," I told her. "The Pym sisters spoke with him as he passed their house. He told them he was going to Dimity Westwood's cottage. I thought you might know him, because of your work with the trust."

Dimity Westwood had been filthy rich, but she hadn't left her capital to gather dust. She'd used a good-sized chunk of it to found the Westwood Trust, an umbrella organization for a number of different charities, of which I was now the titular head.

"You met all sorts of people back then, didn't you?" I asked. "Poor people, I mean."

My work with the trust introduced me to a great number of people I wouldn't otherwise have had the privilege to meet. It certainly broadened my horizons.

Dimity's unspoken reprimand stung, but only slightly. I didn't want to see homeless people on my horizons. When panhandlers came toward me, I ran the other way. And since this particular vagrant had intruded on the first day of my Christmas celebration, I was feeling even less charitable than usual.

"Is it possible that the tramp's a friend of yours?" I asked patiently.

It's more than possible. It's highly probable.

"Why do you say that?" I asked.

He used the bridle path, Lori.

"So?"

The bridle path shaves a quarter-mile from the distance between Finch and my cottage.

The bridle path ran along the edge of the river in Finch, out of sight of most of the houses, then followed a course that crossed behind the Pym sisters' house, wound past the Harrises' stables, and cut through the oak grove that separated my property from theirs.

A stranger wouldn't know about the bridle path. The gentleman must have visited me on previous occasions, and he must have been a regular visitor, to know about such a shortcut.

"He hasn't come here recently, though," I pointed out, "or he would've known that you're . . . no longer at home to visitors."

An old friend, then, out of touch for some years. . . . What would compel a sick and starving man to venture down a lonely bridle path in the midst of a blizzard?

"Does it really matter?" I asked, preoccupied with thoughts of Christmas pudding.

Of course it does. We must do something, Lori.

"He's already in the Radcliffe, getting the best medical care money can buy," I asserted.

But what will happen to him after he's released from hospital? We must find someone to look after him——his family, his friends. . . . He must not, under any circumstances, be thrown back onto the streets.

"But we don't know who he is," I said.

Then we must find out. Describe him to me.

I shrugged. "Tall, thin. Long hair, long beard, both gray."

And his face?

"His face?" I tried to focus on the man's features, but all I could remember was the beard, the hair, and, oddly enough, his long, almost delicate fingers. "He has beautiful hands," I offered. "That's the best I can do. For Pete's sake, Dimity, I was saving a man's life, not painting his portrait."

Then you must go to the Radcliffe and have another look at him.

"Today?" I asked nervously. Hospital visits were not high on my list of favorite activities.

The sooner the better.

"But today's my mother's birthday," I protested. "Bill and I were going to get our family Christmas under way."

Your family Christmas will have to wait, Lori. I'm sure your mother would understand. You must go to the Radcliffe as soon as possible.

"The guy's in a coma," I said.

Then he won't mind being stared at, will he? The handwriting continued more swiftly. *It's no time to be squeamish, Lori. I know how hospitals upset you, but you must go. I cannot bear to think of an old friend lying anonymous and alone in a casualty ward. We must find out who he is.*

"I'll go," I promised grudgingly.

Just remember to breathe through your mouth, dear. A soft

breeze wafted through the study, the ghost of a sigh. *It's a dreadful time of year for the homeless. Winter is not kind to the poor.*

I waited until Aunt Dimity's handwriting had faded from the page, then closed the blue journal and sat for a moment, contemplating the futility of advance planning. I'd planned to spend the day at home with my family, baking angel cookies, hanging ornaments, and belting out my favorite carols, but the tramp's arrival had turned my plans to dust. Thanks to Dimity's disreputable old pal, I'd spend the day in Oxford, trying not to lose my lunch in the Radcliffe's antiseptic corridors.

"Ho. Ho. Ho," I muttered irritably, putting the journal back on the shelf.

Feeling aggrieved, and feeling guilty for feeling aggrieved, I returned to the living room. The Pyms were playing peekaboo with Rob, Bill was giving Will a horsey ride on his knee, and Nell was discussing the Nativity play with Willis, Sr., who was transparently delighted to learn that Nell would be playing Mary to his Joseph.

"Peggy Kitchen coveted the part," Nell was saying as I entered the room, "but even she had to agree that I was more suitable."

I paused midstride, momentarily distracted by the notion of an oversized, bossy widow like Peggy Kitchen playing the role of a round young virgin, then continued across the room to stand in front of the fireplace, where I could speak to everyone at once.

"I'm sorry to interrupt," I said, "but Bill and I have to go to Oxford."

"Oxford?" Bill groaned. "I thought we agreed to spend the next two weeks at home."

"I've had a sudden change of heart," I said, giving him an I'll-explain-everything-later glare. "I'm worried about the tramp. I want to see for myself that he's being looked after properly."

The telephone rang and Bill picked it up.

Ruth firmly endorsed my plan. "One can never be too careful . . ."

". . . when pneumonia sets in," Louise continued. "You might bring him a thermos of strengthening broth or . . ."

". . . a pot of calf's-foot jelly," suggested Ruth.

"How are you going to get to Oxford?" asked Nell. "The lane's drifted in all the way to Finch. I'd offer my sleigh, but—" She broke off, interrupted by a cottage-shaking rumble.

Startled, Willis, Sr., turned to look out of the bow window, but I already knew what he would see. Mr. Barlow's snowplow was a local institution, a home-built monstrosity consisting of a wide blade welded slantwise to the front of a garbage truck. Clouds of dark smoke puffed from its exhaust pipe and its engine roared like a demented dinosaur, but Mr. Barlow, a retired mechanic, had reason to be proud of his creation. Noisy and unsightly though it was, it cleared the country lanes surrounding Finch with an efficiency that put the county to shame.

"There," I said, when the snowplow had passed. "Now we can drive to Oxford."

"I'm not so sure about that," said Bill, hanging up the phone. The look on his face told me that something was terribly wrong. "It's Hyram Collier," he said, in answer to my unspoken question. "He died last night at his home in Boston, of a massive heart attack."

"Oh, Bill, I'm so sorry." Hyram Collier was a millionaire philanthropist whose son had been at boarding school with Bill back in the States. Hyram was the exact opposite of Willis, Sr.—an extravagant extrovert who knew how to make an awkward young boy feel at ease. Hyram had been there to comfort Bill when Bill's mother had died in a foolish traffic accident, and had remained a steadfast source of advice and friendship ever since. "When is the funeral?"

"The day after tomorrow," said Bill. "I should be there, but . . ."

"You'll be there," I said, taking Will from him. "William can drive you to Heathrow this afternoon. You'll be in Boston tomorrow."

"But how will you get to Oxford?" Bill asked.

"Forget about Oxford," I said. It was no time to challenge my husband's erroneous conviction that I was incapable of driving in England. "Just go upstairs and pack."

I felt a vague sense of foreboding as Bill said good-bye to Nell Harris and the Pyms. First the tramp had arrived, and now Bill was leaving.

Christmas was definitely not going as planned.

4

I left for Oxford early the next morning, warmly clad in a claret-colored velvet tunic, slim black wool trousers, and my gorgeous cashmere coat. I paused on the way to pick up a thermos of strengthening broth and a pot of calf's-foot jelly from the Pyms. I knew that the tramp was in no shape to consume the sisters' remedies, but I thought the broth might do me some good. The mere thought of entering a hospital made me weak in the knees.

I was not cut out for the medical profession. The sight of sick people made me feel sick, and I nursed a secret horror of bumbling into dreadful scenes involving protruding bones, gaping wounds, and vats of bodily fluids. I hoped and prayed that I wouldn't disgrace myself on the way to the tramp's bedside.

My car, a Morris Mini that had seen better days, handled the snow-slick lane with surprising ease, and my first glimpse of Finch covered in snow drove away all thoughts of carnage.

The blizzard had turned the village into a frosty fairyland. The golden limestone buildings glowed like honey in the bright morning sun. Twinkling icicles graced each overhanging eave, every roof sported a fine, deep crown of snow, and the holly bushes surrounding the war memorial gleamed as if each leaf had been individually polished. Finch would have looked like a gingerbread village decked out in its winter finery if the villagers had left well enough alone.

They had, alas, entered into the spirit of the season with a display of bad taste that was truly breathtaking. Disembodied plastic Santa heads garroted with tinselly garlands leered from the tearoom's windows, life-sized plastic choirboys alternated with blinking candy canes along the front of Peacock's pub, and the large display window in Kitchen's Emporium featured a deer-shaped lawn ornament posed stiffly beside a motorized Father Christmas whose staring eyes and lurching movements hinted more at madness than at merriment.

"Good grief," I muttered, skidding to a halt in front of the horrible display. "If I'd seen that as a child, I'd've run screaming into the night."

No sooner had I voiced the thought than a truly frightening vision appeared as the front door of the Emporium opened and its proprietress came charging toward my car, shouting, "Lori! I want a word with you!"

Peggy Kitchen—shopkeeper, postmistress, and undisputed empress of Finch—had mellowed somewhat since her engagement to the long-suffering Jasper Taxman, but she still ruled the village with an iron hand. Bill referred to her as a wolf in grandmother's clothing. No one in his right mind would dream of telling Peggy that her window display was likely to give small children nightmares.

Peggy eyed me suspiciously as I rolled down the Mini's

window. "What's all this about you encouraging undesirables to come to the village?"

"Excuse me?" I said.

"They say you plucked a tramp out of the gutter and dropped him in the lap of luxury," Peggy boomed.

I didn't bother asking who "they" were. "They" was village shorthand for the ubiquitous garbled gossip that spread news faster than optic cables.

"I found a sick man and got him to a hospital," I explained.

"In a helicopter," roared Peggy. "Seems the lap of luxury to me."

"The lane was blocked," I pointed out, "and the man was in critical condition."

"Malingering," Peggy said ominously. "You can't trust these fellows. Liars and thieves, all of them."

"Did he steal anything?" I asked.

"Not that I know of," Peggy admitted. "But he must've been up to no good, to come sneaking around here."

"Sneaking?" I said. "What makes you think he was sneaking?"

"No one saw him," Peggy thundered. "He slipped through the village like a thief in the night, which I've no doubt he is."

"I don't have time for this," I snapped, and rolled the window up so quickly that I nearly nipped the tip of Peggy's nose. I wasn't a fan of tramps and vagabonds, but Peggy's blanket condemnation riled me. She had no right to call Aunt Dimity's old friend a thief.

It was odd, though, that no one had seen him. As I left Peggy fuming in the slush, I wondered why he hadn't stopped at Peacock's pub before going on to the cottage. He could have warmed himself at the fire before tackling the long walk, but he chose instead to bypass Finch entirely. It was almost as if, like poor old Robert Anscombe, he hadn't wanted to be seen.

On the other hand, I mused, he might have been playing it safe. I doubted that the Peacocks would have been as harsh as Peggy Kitchen, but they probably wouldn't have encouraged the tramp to sit by their fire for very long. Panhandlers were notoriously bad for business.

I drove past the schoolhouse, where the Nativity play would take place on Christmas Eve, and up Saint George's Lane, where I spotted the vicar trudging toward the church. He waved to me to stop and I pulled over.

Theodore Bunting was so tall that he had to bend nearly double in order to speak to me through the Mini's window. His mournful gray eyes surveyed me sadly as he dabbed at his red nose with a white handkerchief.

"Are you all right, Vicar?" I asked.

"A slight head cold," he replied, sounding as though his head were stuffed with cotton wool. "Lilian and I were very sorry to hear of Bill's loss. He's off to Boston for the funeral, I understand."

Again, I didn't bother to ask the source of the vicar's information. News traveled through the village as swiftly as windblown snow.

"He'll be back on Friday," I informed him.

"Oh, dear." The vicar frowned anxiously. "The first rehearsal of the Nativity play is tomorrow. However will Lilian find another Joseph on such short notice?"

"Bill's father has already volunteered," I said smoothly. "In fact, William would like to take over the role entirely, if it's okay with Lilian."

The vicar's face cleared. "She'll be delighted. God knows she doesn't want Mrs. Kitchen playing Joseph." He sneezed twice, stood to blow his nose, then bent low again. "Lilian told me about the unfortunate gentleman you rescued yesterday. Have you any news of him?"

I'd spoken with Dr. Pritchard before I left the cottage, so I was able to give the vicar an update on the tramp's condition.

"He's still unconscious," I told him, "but he's stable."

"Thank the Lord," the vicar said gravely. "No idea who the fellow is?"

"None," I said. "The police have sent out John Doe bulletins to all of the local shelters, but so far no one's identified him."

The vicar sighed. "Poor chap. I'll offer up a prayer for him at evensong. Mr. Barlow sends his best wishes as well."

"I'll pass them along," I said.

I closed the window, oddly comforted by the vicar's words. It was a relief to know that not everyone in Finch was as narrow-minded as Peggy Kitchen.

Oxford was as unpleasant as ever, noisy and traffic-choked, a lumpy conglomeration of beautiful colleges swallowed whole, but never fully digested, by a sprawling, unkempt town.

The slushy conditions had reduced the usual stream of bicyclists to a trickle, but the swarming hordes of students had been replaced by hordes of holiday shoppers, none of whom seemed to know the most elementary rules of traffic safety. I frightened a good half-dozen pedestrians before finding sanctuary in a parking garage near the Radcliffe.

Dr. Pritchard was with a patient when I arrived at the reception desk, but he'd told Reception to expect me and assigned a round-faced, red-haired student nurse to take me through to intensive care.

Nurse Willoughby was one of those annoying individuals who seem to thrive on the smell of disinfectant. While she bounced merrily along, I kept my eyes trained on her heels and breathed shallowly through my mouth.

"Our patient is in an isolation ward, because of his pneumonia," the young nurse informed me brightly. "He hasn't regained consciousness yet, but that's not necessarily a bad sign. Matron says it may be that his body needs a good, long rest." She turned a broad smile in my direction. "I can understand your interest in him, Ms. Shepherd. He's . . ." The young nurse blushed prettily. "He's really something special. We all think so. Even Matron."

We stopped at a nurses' station overlooking a glass-walled cubicle, and I exchanged my cashmere coat and leather shoulder bag for a wraparound surgical gown and a tie-on surgical mask.

"You see what I mean?" Nurse Willoughby whispered. She motioned toward three nurses standing before the cubicle. "They come here during their breaks, just to get a glimpse of him." Her freckled face became somber. "It's not just that he's handsome," she said gravely. "Anyone can be handsome, but he's got an air about him . . . as if he's come to remind us of why our jobs are so important. We're taking better care of all our patients because of him." She tugged my gown's elastic cuff into place. "But you know what I mean. You've seen him already."

I smiled amiably, even though I hadn't the foggiest notion what Nurse Willoughby meant. The tramp, as I recalled him, had been about as inspirational as a latter-day Howard Hughes.

"You're sure this is the right guy?" I asked. "The elderly man who—"

"Elderly man?" Nurse Willoughby exclaimed. "You can

hardly call our patient elderly, Ms. Shepherd. Dr. Pritchard says he's no more than forty years old."

I stared at her, taken aback. I could scarcely believe that
the gaunt and gray-haired man who'd lain on our sofa was
only a few years older than my husband. "You're sure?"

Nurse Willoughby was positive. "You must've been
fooled by his hair color—prematurely gray, Matron says.
And of course he's so terribly thin. . . . Now," she continued, in a businesslike tone, "Dr. Pritchard's waived the
rules about visiting hours, but you'll still have only ten
minutes with our patient."

"That's fine by me," I told her.

The tramp's admirers dispersed as we approached the
glass-walled cubicle. Nurse Willoughby opened the door,
pulled it shut behind me, and returned to the nurses'
station.

I paused just inside the doorway, gazing once more at
the floor. I wasn't a trained nurse. I didn't find sick people
fascinating. I'd made it through the hospital corridors with
my dignity intact, but coming face-to-face with a critically
ill patient was another matter. Still, I thought, I'd promised Aunt Dimity. . . . I braced myself and lifted my gaze.

The tramp seemed as frail as an autumn leaf. His collarbones stood out in sharp relief against the pale-blue hospital gown, and his long, tapering fingers were hidden
beneath layers of gauze. A clear plastic oxygen mask covered his nose and mouth, IVs snaked from his arms, and
thin wires connected him to a bank of beeping, blinking
machines that loomed at the far side of his bed. His long
hair was clipped short, his shaggy beard shaved off, and an
overhead lamp cast a halo of light upon a face so beautiful
it took my breath away.

He wasn't an old man. I could see that now. His skin was

weathered but taut, his chin firm, and the long lashes casting half-moon shadows on his windburned cheeks were as dark as my own. I took one step, then another, until I stood beside his bed, looking down on a face I'd seen, but hadn't seen. His wide-set eyes and curving lips might have been carved by Michelangelo.

The long, dark lashes fluttered, the eyelids slowly opened, and the cubicle seemed to vanish as I fell into the depths of his violet eyes. In them I glimpsed a soul wiser, braver, and kinder by far than my own, a soul scarred but undaunted by suffering. He gazed at me so trustingly that for a moment I believed I'd come there not merely to observe, but to save him. I stood spellbound, unaware of my surroundings, until he blinked once, twice, smiled as sweetly as a child, and closed his eyes.

Suddenly, Nurse Willoughby was at my side, pointing to her watch. I turned, as if awakened from a dream, and caught sight of a man staring through the cubicle's glass wall. He was tall and well built—in his fifties, I guessed—and dressed all in black: black turtleneck, black jeans, and a black-leather bomber jacket. His fringe of graying hair thinned to peach fuzz on the top of his head and he sported a neatly trimmed goatee. His long, pouchy face and sad brown eyes reminded me strongly of a placid basset hound.

Nurse Willoughby touched my arm and we left the cubicle, the young nurse looking back a dozen times, as if to fix the tramp's features in her memory. I needed no backward glance. The tramp's face was as clear in my mind as Bill's.

"He opened his eyes," I said, as I stripped off the protective clothing.

"Highly unlikely," Nurse Willoughby informed me.

"He opened his eyes and he smiled," I insisted.

"An involuntary reflex, perhaps," she allowed.

"I know what I saw," I stated firmly.

"And I know what the instruments tell me," she replied, with equal firmness. "You want him to be well, Ms. Shepherd. We all do. But wanting something doesn't make it so. Our patient is deeply unconscious. He couldn't possibly respond to your presence or communicate with you in any way." She patted my arm. "It was probably a trick of the light."

She was trying to be kind, but I felt the same frustration I'd felt when well-meaning people told me that my babies' smiles had more to do with gas than with glee. I was about to argue the point further when the man in the black leather jacket approached me.

"Lori Shepherd?" he inquired.

"Yes," I replied.

"Dr. Pritchard told me you'd be along," the man said. "I'm Julian Bright." He put out his hand. "Would you care to come to Cambridgeshire with me?"

5

The request was so preposterous that I didn't know whether to laugh or call for help. "Thank you, Mr. Bright, but I don't usually accept invitations from complete strangers."

"Please, call me Julian," he said, with a reassuring smile. "And believe me when I tell you that my intentions are honorable. I don't intend to make a pass at you—or any other woman, for that matter."

I took in the goatee and the black leather jacket and felt myself blush. "Oh," I said carefully. "I didn't realize." I motioned toward the cubicle, wondering how best to phrase my next question. "Are you . . . *involved* with the man in there?"

The reassuring smile became a broad grin. "I'm not a homosexual, if that's what you're asking. I'm a priest. A Roman Catholic priest. And I am deeply involved with the man in there. I owe him my life."

Nurse Willoughby put her head between us. "I'm sorry, Julian, but you'll have to take your conversation elsewhere." She handed over my coat and shoulder bag. "You know what Matron will say if she finds you blocking the passageway again."

"One moment, please, Nurse Willoughby," said Julian. "I'm in need of a character reference. Would you be so kind as to inform Ms. Shepherd that I'm an honorable gentleman who means her no harm?"

"I'd be happy to." The red-haired nurse tilted her head toward me and said, in a confidential murmur, "He's mad as a March hare."

"That's not exactly—" Julian began, but Nurse Willoughby cut him off.

"He gave up a posh parish to run a doss-house," she told me. "Makes the rounds here every morning, looking for his lost sheep. Matron says he was in line to become bishop, but he threw it all away for a lot of old soaks."

"Pure self-interest," Julian said quickly. "I fully expect to find a a masquerading millionaire among Saint Benedict's drug addicts and drunks."

Nurse Willoughby laughed. "When you do, give him my name, will you? I could do with a few extra bob." She waggled her fingers at us. "Now run along before Matron throws a fit."

"If anyone wants us, we'll be in the cafeteria," said Julian, and before I could object, he took me by the elbow and steered me down the hospital corridor. "Dr. Pritchard told me that you called out the RAF rescue squad for Smitty. I can't tell you how grateful I am. A lot of people would've looked the other way."

"It wasn't really my idea," I confessed, embarrassed by the undeserved praise.

"But you're here now," Julian pointed out. "Not every woman would take time out of her busy holiday schedule to visit a man like Smitty."

I shrugged weakly. "That wasn't my idea, either."

"But you're glad you spent time with him," Julian ventured. "I can see it in your face."

Startled, I lifted a hand to my cheek. Did I look as starstruck as the knot of nurses I'd seen clustered around the tramp's cubicle? "Is his name really Smitty or is it just a nickname?"

"It's what we call him at Saint Benedict's," Julian replied.

We entered a brightly lit, cheerfully painted cafeteria that seemed to cater to patients, staff, and visitors alike. Almost everyone in the room called a greeting to Julian as he escorted me to a corner table.

"Cup of tea?" he asked.

"Yes, please." I folded my coat over the chair next to mine and rested my arms on the table, feeling as though I'd been washed ashore by a minor tidal wave. Julian Bright might look like a placid basset hound, but he had the energy of a fox terrier. He paused at a dozen tables on his way to the tea urn, fielding questions, tossing off quips, and at one point kneeling on the floor to speak quietly with a young girl in a wheelchair. I needed no further proof that he was indeed the honorable gentleman he claimed to be.

As I waited for my tea, a flock of questions flitted through my mind. How well did Julian know Smitty? Had the tramp really saved his life? Above all, why would a Catholic priest invite me to go with him to Cambridgeshire?

Julian returned with three cups of tea on a blue plastic tray. He placed two of the cups in front of me, set aside the third for himself, hung his black leather jacket on the back of his chair, and sat opposite me.

I pointed to the pair of teacups. "Why two?"

"To help you recover from the shock of meeting me." He added milk to his tea and stirred. "I'm afraid I got rather ahead of myself back there. It's just that it's my night to supervise dinner at Saint Benedict's, which means that I have to leave for Cambridgeshire in less than an hour. I'd very much like you to come with me."

"Why?" I asked.

"To help Smitty find the specialized care he'll need once he leaves here." Julian laid his spoon aside. "Unless you're willing to take him in."

"Er, I, uh . . ." I sipped my tea and fumbled for an answer. "I hadn't planned on it."

"I can't do it, either," said Julian. "Saint Benedict's is no place for a man with his sort of illness."

"What is Saint Benedict's?" I asked.

"A hostel for transient men—a homeless shelter, if you will," Julian replied. "It's tucked in among the council estates in East Oxford. I don't expect you get there much."

"And you work there?" I said.

"I run the place," said Julian.

I leaned forward. "Don't you feed the men who come to you?"

"Of course we do," Julian said.

"Then why is Smitty half-dead from starvation?" I demanded. Several heads turned in my direction, and I lowered my voice to an outraged murmur. "Did you see him? He's like a scarecrow, hardly a scrap of flesh on him."

Julian lowered his eyes for a moment, then regarded me steadily. "We provide food for the men," he said, "but we can't force them to eat it. Smitty had every opportunity to avail himself of simple, nourishing meals while he was at Saint Benedict's, but he apparently chose instead to starve himself." He bowed his head. "I'm ashamed to say that I was unaware of his condition until Dr. Pritchard told me of it this morning."

I sat back, disarmed by the priest's confession. I recalled the layers of ragged clothing and the oversized greatcoat

Smitty had worn, and realized that Julian would have needed X-ray vision to see the gaunt form beneath the baggy costume. I hadn't realized Smitty's frailty until I'd helped Bill carry him into the cottage.

"I'm sorry," I said stiffly. "I spoke without thinking, as usual. It's just, seeing Smitty like that . . . his hands . . ."

"Frostbite," said Julian. "The good news is that they probably won't have to be amputated."

I groaned softly and pushed my second cup of tea to one side.

"And please," Julian continued, "don't apologize for caring about someone as vulnerable as Smitty. As you so rightly point out, he's terribly ill. I believe there may be some form of dementia involved."

"You think he's crazy?" I said, vaguely offended by the notion.

"I suspect so, but I can't be completely certain. That's why I'm going to Cambridgeshire. One of the men at Saint Benedict's told me that Smitty lived there before coming to Oxford. He worked at a place called Blackthorne Farm for over a year. The farm's owned by a widow named Anne Preston. She must have gotten to know Smitty fairly well while he worked for her."

"And if Anne Preston thinks he's crazy, it'll be two against one," I said sourly.

"I'm not inventing Smitty's symptoms, Ms. Shepherd," said Julian. "He elected to starve himself, and . . . Here, have a look at this." He reached into his jacket pocket and pulled out a water-stained suede pouch.

"What is it?" I said, eyeing the pouch curiously.

"Nurse Willoughby found it in Smitty's coat pocket," said Julian. "She didn't want it to disappear into an orderly's pocket, so she gave it to me for safekeeping. Nurse Willoughby thought the contents might be valuable."

"Are they?" I asked.

"I'll leave it to you to judge." Julian teased open the pouch's drawstring and turned it upside down over the table, releasing a colorful cascade of military decorations—ribbons, medals, bars, and a slender golden eagle with widespread wings.

My pulse quickened at the sight of the golden eagle. Aunt Dimity had been engaged to a fighter pilot who'd been killed in the Battle of Britain. Perhaps the medals belonged to someone Dimity had known during the war. Smitty might have come to the cottage on behalf of an aging airman.

"A DSO," said Julian, separating one medal from the pile. "The Distinguished Service Order, given to commissioned officers of the navy, army, and air force for special distinction in action. The bar means that the airman won the medal twice over."

My ears pricked up. "How do you know it was given to an airman?"

Instead of answering me directly, Julian proceeded to identify two other medals. "The Distinguished Flying Cross, awarded for gallantry when flying in an engagement against an enemy. The Air Force Cross, given for acts of courage when flying in any context other than combat."

I lifted the golden eagle from the table. "And this?"

"The Pathfinder badge," Julian replied. "Pathfinders were the crème de la crème, members of an elite corps culled from the best bomber crews in the Royal Air Force."

"Bombers," I echoed thoughtfully, placing the golden eagle on the table. Dimity had never said a word to me about bomber crews, but she'd known so many people during the war that anything was possible.

Julian plucked at his goatee worriedly as he stared down at the medals. "Smitty left all of his possessions at

Saint Benedict's—except for the items you see before you. Would a sane man undertake such a difficult journey with nothing in his pockets but a pouchful of old military decorations?"

I answered his question with a question. "Did Smitty ever mention a woman named Dimity Westwood?"

"The philanthropist?" Julian shook his head. "He said nothing to me about her. She's dead, isn't she?"

"Yes," I said, restraining the urge to add *more or less*. "I know a lot about her, though. She used to live in my cottage."

"So Smitty collapsed at Dimity Westwood's cottage." Julian shrugged. "Could be pure coincidence."

"Dimity was engaged to a fighter pilot during the war," I informed him. "She got to know a lot of airmen. Smitty might have been bringing the medals to her—not knowing she was dead—on behalf of someone she knew back then."

"But who?" said Julian. "And why the urgency?"

I looked down at the table. "I don't know."

"Nor do I." Julian paused. "But Anne Preston might." He held out his hand imploringly. "Please, Ms. Shepherd, come with me. It'll take us two hours to get to Blackthorne Farm and two hours to return. You'll be home in plenty of time for your evening meal."

"Why do you need me?" I asked, puzzled by his persistence.

"Because you care about Smitty," said Julian. "Because Anne Preston may say things to you that she wouldn't feel comfortable saying to me." He hesitated, then plunged on. "And because I'm a Roman Catholic priest. We aren't always welcomed with open arms in this country."

"But—" I started to say "you don't even look like a priest," realized how foolish it would sound, and changed it to "I've got two children waiting for me at home."

The priest cocked his head to one side. "On their own, are they?"

"Don't be silly," I said, smiling. "My father-in-law's taking care of them."

"And he'll fall to pieces if you arrive home a few hours later than expected?" Julian prodded.

"No," I said, "but—"

"Please." Julian reached across the table and clasped my hands in his. "We'll be back in Oxford by four o'clock, at the latest. You may have two children at home, but I have a hundred and fifty men to feed."

I could feel myself weakening. Dimity had ordered me to find Smitty's family or friends, but her orders meant less to me at that moment than the look of trust I'd seen in those violet eyes. I felt I had to do something to confirm Smitty's faith in me. Perhaps, I thought, I should go along to Blackthorne Farm, to keep this priest from railroading a defenseless man into an asylum.

I looked down at Julian's hands and noted, with a faint sense of disquiet, that they were nearly as beautiful as Smitty's. I gently pulled away from him and began gathering up the medals. "Have you tried telephoning Blackthorne Farm?"

"Yes," said Julian, "but the lines are down because of the storm."

I gave an exasperated snort. "If the lines are down, the roads are probably impassable. I drive a Mini, Julian. It doesn't do snowdrifts. How are we going to get through?"

"Have faith, my child." Triumph gleamed in Julian's brown eyes as he tucked the suede pouch into his pocket. "Saint Christopher will provide."

6

Julian Bright's khaki-colored Land Rover looked as though it belonged in intensive care, alongside Smitty. Julian claimed that the vehicle's multiple contusions proved its worth, but I was better reassured by a brand-new set of snow tires and a well-oiled winch mounted on the front bumper.

Julian patted the dashboard proudly as he pulled away from the parking garage. "Got him in Mombasa."

"Not much snow in Mombasa," I observed. "And aren't vehicles generally referred to as 'she'?"

"Not when they're christened Saint Christopher." Julian flipped a lever on the dashboard and a blast of heat erupted from the vents.

"At least we won't freeze to death when we're stranded in a snowbank," I commented.

Julian rolled his eyes heavenward. "O ye of little faith."

I pulled my cellular phone from my coat pocket and telephoned Willis, Sr. He was, as I'd expected, unfazed by the change of plans. He passed along the news that Bill had arrived safely in Boston, and by the time we finished our conversation, I was fairly certain that my father-in-law was pleased as Punch to have Bill and me out from underfoot and his grandsons all to himself.

The sun was shining brightly, but a brisk wind buffeted the Land Rover as we escaped the clinging tentacles of Oxford. Blackthorne Farm lay somewhere in the vicinity of a village called Great Gransden, about twenty miles west of Cambridge. There was no direct route—there seldom was, in England—but Julian had worked out a series of jigs and jogs that were likely to get us there in two hours, barring the odd snowdrift.

A dazzling white counterpane of snow blanketed the land in all directions, but—luckily for us—an army of snowplows had been at work and the main roads were clear. I donned my sunglasses and sat with Julian's well-thumbed road atlas open in my lap, waiting for him to ask for directions.

"What were you doing in Mombasa?" I asked.

"I thought I wanted to be a missionary," Julian replied, "but the water changed my mind. There comes a time when dysentery ceases to amuse."

I smiled. There was no denying that Julian was good company.

"Come now," he went on, a teasing note in his voice, "aren't you going to ask why I became a priest? It's usually the first thing people want to know."

"I'm familiar with the concept of vocations," I said dryly. "I was raised Catholic."

"You jest," said Julian, giving me a sidelong glance.

"I was born to an Irish Catholic mother on the west side of Chicago," I informed him.

The priest released a heartfelt sigh, murmuring, "Thank heavens."

"Why do you sound so relieved?" I asked.

"Because you know the drill," Julian replied. "I won't have to spend half the journey answering silly questions."

"Such as?"

Julian raised a finger in the air. "Why do I worship statues? Is there a secret tunnel between the convent and the rectory? If the Pope ordered me to kill a child—"

"Do people really say things like that to you?" I broke in, incredulous.

"They do," said Julian, nodding to emphasize his words. "And when it comes to the subject of celibacy—"

"I can imagine," I said quickly. I was beginning to see what a Catholic priest in a Protestant country was up against. "Is that why you don't wear your clerical collar? To avoid . . . unnecessary confrontations?"

A shadow crossed Julian's face. His hand drifted briefly to the collar of his black turtleneck, then came to rest once more on the steering wheel. "Not exactly," he said, his eyes never leaving the road.

I, too, fixed my eyes on the road, disturbed by his sudden stillness. I'd evidently touched on a sensitive subject, and I wasn't sure what to say next. "It must be fascinating," I ventured, "to run a place like Saint Benedict's."

"It's a treat, compared to Mombasa." Julian cleared his throat and gave me a shy smile, as if to apologize for his brief withdrawal. "For one thing, the water's a good deal easier on my digestive system."

"Is it true, what Nurse Willoughby said, about you becoming a bishop?"

"Nurse Willoughby was, as usual, overstating the case." He relaxed his grip on the steering wheel and settled back in the driver's seat. "I was a bishop's secretary until I began to question the dispersal of certain church funds. The bishop decided that since I was so fond of the poor, I should be sent to work among them. Hence, my posting to Saint Benedict's."

"So Saint Benedict's is a punishment," I said.

"A gift," Julian countered. "I'm not cut out for administrative work."

Or hypocrisy, I thought. I closed the atlas and tucked it into the map pocket on the door, then wiped a hand across my damp forehead. The heat had become so oppressive that I was tempted to strip down to the silk camisole I wore beneath my velvet tunic, but settled for unbuttoning my cashmere coat.

"Did Smitty really save your life?" I asked.

"It's how he introduced himself to me." Julian flipped the visor down to reduce the glare and made a slight adjustment to the rearview mirror. "A month ago, a fight erupted in the dining room at Saint Benedict's. When I tried to break it up, a chap called Bootface seized a knife and threatened to carve me up like an underdone steak."

"Jesus!" I exclaimed, and immediately regretted my choice of words.

Julian's eyes lit with amusement. "I, too, did some fast praying. As it happens, my prayers were answered."

"How?" I asked.

"Smitty walked in," Julian told me. "He'd only just arrived. He dropped his gear on the floor, took a look round, and began straightening the chairs and tables that had been knocked over during the brawl, as if to draw Bootface's attention away from me."

"What did Bootface do?"

"He went mad," said Julian. "He charged at Smitty like an enraged bear." The priest looked over at me. "I'll wager you can't guess what Smitty did."

"Did he run for his life?" I said.

"He smiled." The priest shook his head bemusedly. "That's all. Just smiled. Bootface was so taken aback that he dropped the knife. Two of the men got hold of him and kept him still until the police came to take him away. We don't take death threats lightly at Saint Benedict's."

"Let me get this straight." I folded my leg beneath me and turned sideways on the seat. "A knife-wielding maniac came charging at Smitty, and all Smitty did was smile?"

"I asked him about it after the police had gone," Julian said. "He told me he'd simply done the first thing that came to mind. I found his response quite disturbing."

"I thought you were supposed to advocate turning the other cheek," I said.

"There's a vast difference between turning one's cheek and sticking one's neck out." Julian pursed his lips. "I'm grateful that he saved my life, but I'd rather he hadn't risked his own in the process." Julian fell silent as he negotiated a roundabout, and when he spoke again, his voice had lost its customary carefree lilt. "I feel the same way about his needless abstinence, though I may be partially to blame for it."

"How do you figure that?" I asked.

"Smitty came into the office one night and found me worrying over our accounts," said Julian. "He asked what was wrong and I'm afraid I told him more than I should have. It's possible that he skimped on meals in order to save Saint Benedict's money."

"Is Saint Benedict's in financial trouble?" I asked.

"No more than usual." Julian straightened his shoulders

and mustered a smile. "Did I mention how grateful I am to you for coming with me to Blackthorne Farm?"

I recognized an evasion when I heard one, but by then I was too hot to care. I swung forward in my seat. "I think I'm melting, Julian. Could we have a little less heat, please?"

"Ah, yes, about the heat . . ." Julian went on to explain, somewhat sheepishly, that since Saint Christopher's heating system possessed no sense of subtlety, our choices were limited to freezing or broiling.

I didn't relish the thought of freezing, so I took off my coat and tossed it into the backseat, next to a beat-up khaki-colored canvas carryall.

"What's in the bag?" I asked. "Emergency rations?"

"Your lack of faith in my trusty vehicle is beginning to distress me, Ms. Shepherd," said Julian. "Saint Christopher is the patron saint of travelers. He won't let us down."

"He's been demoted, hasn't he?" Julian gave me a withering glance and I added hastily, "Sorry. No more cracks about Saint Christopher, I promise. And please, call me Lori."

"Thank you, Lori." Mollified, Julian returned his attention to the road ahead. "The bag is Smitty's. I brought it along to prove our bona fides to Anne Preston."

I regarded the bag with fresh interest. It was creased and faded, as though it had traveled a long way. "Shouldn't you turn it over to the police?"

"The police are far too busy to take an interest in men like Smitty," Julian stated firmly. "If I give it to them, they'll tuck it away in an evidence room and it will never again see the light of day."

"Have you looked through it?" I asked.

"Yes," said Julian. "I thought it might contain a vital piece of information about Smitty—where he comes from, his proper name, that sort of thing—but I found nothing of the sort." He glanced at me hopefully. "Would you care to have a look? You may see something I missed."

I hesitated. I didn't like the thought of rifling through Smitty's belongings without his permission.

Julian seemed to read my mind. "As long as Smitty can't speak for himself," he said quietly, "his possessions must speak for him."

I reached for the bag. As I pulled the canvas carryall into my lap, I had the same sensation I'd had when Bill and I had carried Smitty into the cottage. The bag was far too light. It didn't seem big enough to hold everything a man owned.

The main compartment held practical items: spare socks and underclothing, a tin mug, a soup spoon, a pocketknife, and a white towel in a plastic bag. A side pocket held nothing but a dog-eared prayer book and a loop of braided straw. There was no address book, no scrawled name on a scrap of paper, not even a set of initials penciled on the prayer book's flyleaf. The carryall's contents seemed as anonymous as their owner.

I took up the loop of braided straw. It was exquisite, pale gold and intricately woven in coils and curlicues, with the faint scent of autumn still clinging to its intertwining strands.

"A corn dolly," I said. "That's what it's called in the States, anyway. I think it has something to do with—" I fell silent as an interesting thought occurred to me.

"In this country," Julian informed me, "it's regarded as a fertility symbol. Or a love token."

"It's the same at home." I held the loop up to catch the sunlight. What was a love token doing among Smitty's scant possessions? Had Anne Preston presented her hired hand with a symbol of something more than simple friendship? "I wonder why Smitty left Blackthorne Farm," I said. "Do you think he and Anne Preston were, uh—"

"*Involved?*" Julian said, with exaggerated emphasis. "We'll soon find out." He flashed a grin and pressed down on the accelerator.

The Cotswolds' gently rolling hills gradually gave way to the Midlands' broad, flat plains. Snow-covered fields stretched out to the horizon, sliced into vast, irregular tiles by windbreaks and hedges. The broad vistas were broken by an occasional copse of trees—survivors of the dense forests that had once blanketed the region—and thin trails of blue smoke rising from the chimneys of distant farmhouses. I noted a line of dark clouds building in the west but, remembering my promise to Julian, kept my fears about the weather to myself.

We were traveling the side roads now, and Saint Christopher was performing admirably, churning through windblown drifts without a skid or a hint of hesitation. Julian paused briefly in a lay-by, to compare a scribbled set of directions to the road map in the atlas, then drove on.

"We're nearly there," he said.

Famous last words, I thought, but ten minutes later we were cruising up a snow-packed drive lined with majestic blackthorn hedges.

Blackthorne Farm was a curious amalgam of the romantic and the utilitarian. The farmhouse was a charming Tudor jumble of tiled roofs, half-timbered walls, and mullioned windows, and the stables looked very much as they would have looked three hundred years before. The barn, on the other hand, was sheathed in corrugated iron and linked to two huge metal silos, and the machine shed was nothing more than an enormous fiberglass box.

There was a pleasing air of prosperity about the place. The outbuildings were well tended, the fences in good repair, and the stable yard was immaculate. Anne Preston, it seemed, had a knack for farming.

No sooner had Julian switched off the engine than the front door opened and a pair of frisky black-and-white border collies trotted out, followed by a fair-haired young man.

"Branwell! Charlotte!" he called, and the dogs came to heel at his side.

"Branwell?" I muttered. "Charlotte? I thought Brontë country was further north."

"Brontë country is a state of mind," Julian said sternly. "Now behave yourself. We're here on serious business." He took the canvas carryall from me and we both got out of the car. The stable yard's earthy scent wafted through the crisp, cold air and I heard a horse's whinny as we approached the house.

"Can I help you?" the young man inquired. He appeared to be in his mid-twenties, tall and sturdily built, with a bull neck and broad shoulders beneath a bulky fisherman's sweater.

"We were hoping to speak with Anne Preston," said Julian, stopping a few feet from the doorstep. "I understand she lives here."

The young man smiled. "She's Anne Somerville now," he informed us proudly. "I'm Charles Somerville. We were married three weeks ago."

"Congratulations," Julian said heartily. "Is Mrs. Somerville in?"

It was clear that the novelty of hearing the words *Mrs. Somerville* had not yet worn off. Charles flushed with pleasure as he turned to shout over his shoulder, "Anne! Anne, you have visitors!"

A moment later, a petite, dark-haired woman came to the door. Her raven hair hung thick and straight to her jawline, framing a creamy complexion and a pair of arresting green eyes. She was stylishly dressed in well-cut twill trousers, square-toed leather boots, and a charcoal-gray cowl-neck sweater made of the softest angora.

"Mrs. Somerville?" Julian asked.

"Yes," said the woman, in a pleasantly husky voice. "I'm Anne Somerville. Have you come about the rape?"

Julian blanched. "P-pardon?"

"The rapeseed," said Anne Somerville. "I'm expecting a delivery of—" She broke off abruptly and gave a small gasp as she caught sight of the canvas carryall. *"Kit . . ."* she whispered, and without further warning fell, fainting, into her new husband's strong arms.

7

Charles Somerville placed his wife gently on a low settee in the farmhouse's front parlor. A wood fire crackled in the hearth, casting a flickering light on the oak-paneled walls and the jewel-hued Persian rugs layered over the carpeted floor.

The sharp tang of pine mingled with the mellow scent of wood smoke. A cut-glass decanter rested on a bed of evergreen boughs atop a Jacobean sideboard, and a Christmas tree stood between the two mullioned windows, bright with glittering ornaments, a host of tiny white lights, and a quivering waterfall of tinsel.

Branwell and Charlotte lay side by side on the hearth rug, their ears cocked forward, their eyes on their mistress's face. Julian and I sat in a pair of velvet armchairs separated by a low walnut table, looking on helplessly.

"I'm so sorry," Julian murmured, wringing his hands. "I'd no idea she'd react so strongly."

"Why shouldn't she?" Charles caressed his wife's forehead. "Kit saved her life."

"I'm not even sure we're speaking of the same man." Julian motioned toward the canvas carryall at his feet. "The bag belongs to a man who calls himself Smitty."

"His name's Kit Smith. He worked here for a time." Charles looked over his shoulder at Julian. "Is he dead?"

"No," said Julian.

"Do you hear, darling?" Charles turned back to his wife. "Kit's all right."

Anne's eyelids fluttered. "Kit?" she said weakly.

"Kit's fine," said her husband.

Anne inhaled deeply and raised a hand to her temple. With her husband's help, she swung her legs over the side of the settee and pulled herself into a sitting position.

"Brandy," said Charles, and went to the sideboard to fill a glass from the gleaming decanter.

Anne pushed her dark hair back from her pale face and looked directly at Julian Bright. "Kit's not fine, is he," she said flatly.

Julian shook his head. "No, he's not. He's extremely ill."

"I knew it," said Anne. "When he didn't come to the wedding—"

"Here, darling, drink this." Charles sat beside his wife and put the glass of brandy in her hands.

She sipped the amber liquid, paused to catch her breath, then said, without preamble, "Tell me what happened to Kit."

A tumult of emotions played across her face as Julian and I told our separate stories. Her green eyes blazed with anger, widened in alarm, and finally filled with tears, which she dashed away impatiently with the back of her hand. When we'd finished, she sat quite still, staring into the fire. Then she turned to me.

"Thank you for helping Kit," she said. "I'm afraid I don't

know why he came to your cottage. He never mentioned Dimity Westwood while he was at Blackthorne Farm."

Julian took the suede pouch from his pocket and spilled the glittering medals onto the walnut table. "Did he ever speak of these? He had them with him when he went to Lori's cottage."

Anne's grip on the brandy glass tightened. "I've never seen them before. But I'm not surprised to hear that he had them with him. Another symptom of his illness."

"His illness?" I said.

"Illness, mania, obsession . . ." Anne shrugged. "I'm not familiar with the technical term."

"Can you describe the rest of his symptoms?" asked Julian.

"I can do better than that." Anne looked at her husband, who rose from the settee and left the room. A moment later he returned, a small white card in his hand.

"We found this in his room the day after he left," Charles said. "It must have fallen from his bag when he was packing. Something else he never mentioned."

He placed the laminated card atop the scattered medals. Kit Smith's eyes, obscured by long hair, peered up at me from a photo ID issued by the Heathermoor Asylum for the Mentally Disturbed.

It was as if he'd thrown a snake into my lap. I recoiled and shook my head vehemently. "It's a fake," I declared. "Or . . . or maybe he worked there."

Anne Somerville's laugh held no trace of humor. "What reputable institution would hire someone like Kit?"

"You hired him, didn't you?" I snapped.

"Yes, but that was . . . different." Anne turned toward her husband. "Charles," she said brightly, "I believe we could all do with a cup of tea, and perhaps some sandwiches. Would you please see what Mrs. Monroe's left us? The housekeeper," she added, for our benefit. "She's spending the holidays with her grandchildren."

When Charles had gone, Anne placed her empty glass on the sideboard and came to stand before me.

"You don't want to believe that Kit's insane," she said. "I know just how you feel. I didn't want to believe it either." She pointed to the laminated ID card. "But we must face facts."

"What facts?" I scooped up the medals and slid them back into the suede pouch, aware that I was overreacting, but unable to stop myself. "You don't know why Kit carried that card. Haven't you ever heard of fake IDs? Maybe it's some sort of sick joke."

Anne tilted her head to one side. "So he's gotten to you, too," she murmured.

I looked away, disconcerted. "I don't know what you're talking about."

"Don't you?" Anne's mouth curved upward in a strange, sad smile. "Then let me tell you about Kit. For your sake, as well as his."

"Go ahead," I said gruffly, but I knew even as I spoke that nothing she said would convince me that the man I'd seen in the Radcliffe was crazy.

"In order to tell you about Kit," Anne began, "I must tell you a bit about myself." She paced slowly toward the fire, then turned to face Julian and me. "My first husband died of a stroke five years ago. He was thirty-two, and I was six months pregnant with our first child. I went into premature labor and lost the baby." She knelt on the hearth rug and put an arm around Branwell. "It was a terrible time."

"I'm sorry," said Julian, somehow managing to make the clichéd phrase sound sincere.

"Blackthorne Farm was my late husband's dream, not

mine," Anne continued. "I'd no idea how to manage it, but I refused to give it up. It was all I had left of him."

Julian nodded sympathetically.

"As you can imagine, the place soon began to go to pieces," said Anne. "I was on the verge of selling out when I found Kit."

"Found him?" I said.

"He was in the church at Great Gransden, standing before the memorial window." Anne gave Branwell's chin a rub and sat back on her heels. "At first I thought he was an old airman—"

"Why would you think that?" I interrupted.

"The window's dedicated to the bomber crews who flew from the airbase at Gransden Lodge during the war." She closed her eyes, spread her hands upon her thighs, and recited from memory, " 'The people of these villages cared for the airmen who flew from R.A.F. Gransden Lodge. They watched for them and prayed for them.' " Anne's eyes opened and she smiled briefly. "My father made me learn the inscription by heart. He flew as a navigator during the war."

"What was Kit doing in the church?" I asked.

"He said he'd gone inside to escape the rain," Anne replied. "His voice is . . . magical. I kept him talking just to hear it. When he said he was looking for work and a place to stay, I offered him my spare room and a job." A faint blush stained Anne's creamy complexion, but she continued in a level voice. "He was terribly kind, you see, and I was vulnerable."

"How long ago was this?" I asked, a merciless inquisitor.

"Kit moved into the farmhouse just over year ago," Anne answered. "I paid him next to nothing, yet in one short year he turned the place around—and taught me how to manage it. He said he'd learned about farming from his late father, who'd owned a vast estate."

"Did you believe him?" Julian asked.

"Oh, yes," said Anne. "It was clear to me from the start that Kit wasn't just another itinerant farm laborer. It worried me, in fact."

"Why?" asked Julian.

Anne lifted her hands into the air, then let them fall. "Kit dressed in rags. He carried everything he owned in one small bag. He ate like a sparrow and worked like a dog, but it was all a charade. Any fool could tell he'd been born to money. You had only to hear him speak to know he was too well educated, too cultivated to settle for a life of ill-paid drudgery. . . .

"But that's not the only thing that worried me." She got to her feet and returned to the settee. "Kit had one day free every week. On his free days he rose at dawn and drove off in the farm lorry. He never said where he was going and never mentioned his trips once he returned."

"It must have driven you crazy," I put in, wincing slightly at my choice of words.

"It piqued my curiosity," Anne admitted. "So much so that one day, I stowed away in the back of the lorry." Anne blushed and looked down at the floor, as though embarrassed by the memory of her actions.

"Where did he go?" Julian asked.

Anne raised her eyes. "He drove to an abandoned bomber base, a remnant of the war. Cambridgeshire is littered with them, but until then I'd only seen them from a distance." She ran her tongue over her lips, as though her mouth had suddenly gone dry. "I didn't much like the one we went to."

I leaned toward her, fascinated. "What did Kit do when he got there?"

Anne favored me with a level gaze. "He stood at one end of the runway. In the pouring rain. Without moving. For eight hours."

A chill touched my spine and I looked toward the fire, trying to envision the scene as Anne Somerville had described it. I could imagine Kit's long-legged stride as he wound his way between clusters of crumbling bunkers and long-abandoned huts. If I closed my eyes I could see him standing on a cracked and weed-choked runway, his great-coat billowing in the cold wind, his long hair streaming with rain.

"He did the same thing the following week, and the week after that," Anne went on, hammering her point home. "When I finally told him that I'd followed him, and asked what he was doing, do you know what he said?" Tears trembled like ice crystals on the tips of her lashes. "He said, 'I'm keeping watch for the airmen.' "

I looked past Anne Somerville, past the shining Christmas tree, to the farmyard beyond the mullioned windows. The dark clouds I'd seen on the horizon were moving over Blackthorne Farm, and the brilliant sunshine that had followed us all day was growing weaker. In a few more hours dusk would settle over the broad, flat fields, and perhaps another blizzard would close in, but I was no longer afraid for my own safety. I was too filled with fear for Kit.

A tear spilled down Anne's cheek. "Kit's mad," she said. "He's obsessed with war or death or . . ." She paused. "It's probably what drew him to me. He must have sensed that death and I had become old friends."

Julian crossed to Anne's side. "Mrs. Somerville, if this is

too difficult for you, you needn't go on. I think you've told us enough."

"Let her finish." Charles stood in the doorway, gazing at his wife. "Tell them the rest, Anne."

Anne wiped her eyes and straightened her shoulders, seeming to draw strength from her husband's presence. "When Kit told me about the airmen, I knew for certain that he was ill, but by then I didn't care. I'd have done anything to protect him."

"Because you were in love with him?" Julian said gently.

"Me? In love with Kit?" Anne gave an astonished laugh. "I think not. It would've been like falling in love with a monk. Besides," she added, gazing fondly at her husband, "I was too busy falling in love with the manager Kit had taken on."

Charles returned his wife's fond gaze. "Anne thought her heart was dead and buried, but Kit brought it back to life. He made her care about someone other than herself, you see. By the time I showed up, she was ready to fall in love."

Anne's smile dimmed. "Kit saved me as well as my farm. I've thought of him every day since he left. He's a good, kind man, but he simply can't be trusted to look after himself. He needs supervision."

"I agree," said Julian. "That's why Lori and I came to Blackthorne Farm. We were hoping . . ."

I listened with a growing sense of outrage as Julian, Anne, and Charles discussed plans for Kit Smith's future. They didn't talk about providing for his needs until his health was fully restored, but about taking him into a kind of protective custody. If they had their way, Kit would spend the rest of his days confined at Blackthorne Farm, under a comfortable, caring form of house arrest. The

idea made my skin crawl, but the worst part was that Kit
had no voice in the proceedings. What if he didn't want
to return to the farm? Would the invitation become an
ultimatum?

The military medals bit into my palm as I clutched the
soft suede pouch. Kit peered up at me from the Heathermoor Asylum ID, and I gazed back at him, bewildered by
the intensity of my emotions. Kit had smiled at a knife-
wielding lunatic; he'd starved himself; he'd stood on abandoned runways, keeping watch for long-dead airmen.
There was no reason to believe that he was sane.

Yet I knew as surely as I knew my sons' names that the
soul I'd glimpsed behind those violet eyes wasn't that of a
madman.

When Charles brought in the sandwiches, Julian ate
heartily, but I scarcely managed a crust. I could sense
Anne's gaze on me throughout the meal, and when Julian
and I were getting ready to leave, she took me aside.

"I do know what you're feeling," she said, "but you
mustn't let yourself be beguiled by Kit. He's a sick man.
He needs special care."

"Why don't you call the Heathermoor Asylum?" I muttered. "I'm sure they'll be happy to have him back."

Anne's green eyes blazed. "If you think I could do such a
thing, then you haven't heard a word I've said." She turned
to go, but I caught her by the arm.

"I—I'm sorry, Anne," I faltered. "I shouldn't have spoken so harshly. You've been . . . more than kind."

The anger drained from her face, to be replaced by
something resembling pity. "He'll break your heart," she
said, too softly for the others to hear. "The same way he
broke mine."

Snowflakes danced in the headlights as Saint Christopher carried us back to Oxford. It was scarcely three o'clock, but the sun was already low on the horizon. Pinpricks of light dotted the plains as lamps were lit in isolated farmsteads, then winked out, one by one, as a swirling cape of snow swept across the open plains.

I put the suede pouch in Kit's carryall and kept the battered bag on my lap. As dusk closed in around us, I thought of him lying in the Radcliffe, haloed by golden light, dreaming of a war that had been over for half a century.

"Charles and Anne are a lovely couple," Julian said brightly.

I made no comment.

"The Somervilles are going to visit Kit tomorrow," Julian continued. "I'll have to remember to tell Dr. Pritchard to expect them."

"Good idea," I said, gazing down at the canvas bag.

A few miles passed before Julian observed, "You're awfully quiet, Lori."

"Am I?" I thought for a moment, then shrugged. "I guess I don't have much to say."

Julian sighed. "It's not easy to accept, I know, but it explains a lot, don't you think?"

"No," I said bluntly.

"Then tell me how he ended up at Saint Benedict's," Julian challenged. "How did the son of a prosperous landowner come to live among drunks and drug addicts? Why did he smile when Bootface tried to kill him? Why did he choose to go hungry in the midst of plenty?"

I toyed with the tab on the carryall's zipper while I gave Julian's questions careful consideration. "As a priest," I said finally, "you should know better than most people that there's another way to look at Kit's behavior."

"Go on," said Julian.

"Kit comes from a comfortable home," I said, gazing out at the falling snow, "yet he chooses to live among the poor. He befriends outcasts. When faced with violence, he turns the other cheek. He gives up his own meals—sacrifices himself—so that others may eat." I smoothed the canvas carryall with my palms. "If Kit's crazy, then Christ was crazy, too."

"Ah, I see." Julian stroked his goatee meditatively. "You think Kit might be a religious fanatic."

"I think Kit's a good man!" I exclaimed heatedly. "And the world's in a pretty sorry state if we've started classifying goodness as a form of mental illness."

Julian gave me a sharp glance, then faced forward. "Christ didn't stand in the rain watching invisible airplanes," he said. "And Christ was never confined to an asylum."

I let the words flow over me, unheeded. I couldn't explain all of Kit's behavior. I didn't know for sure why he'd gone to the airfields, or the Heathermoor Asylum.

But I intended to find out.

I returned home to find my sons on the living-room floor, surrounded by empty cardboard boxes—their favorite toys—while my father-in-law, immaculate as ever, watched over them from the comfort of a nearby armchair. After greeting Will and Rob, and covertly scanning them for signs of damage, I sat on the floor with them and filled Willis, Sr., in on my very eventful day. I expected my eminently sensible father-in-law to fall in line with popular opinion on the subject of Kit Smith's sanity, but, as usual, he surprised me.

"The evidence is flimsy at best," he pronounced. "Mr. Smith's actions, in my opinion, remain open to interpretation. We cannot know for certain what he meant when he told Mrs. Somerville that he was 'keeping watch for the airmen.' Perhaps he was speaking metaphorically. Perhaps he was being facetious, in an attempt to discourage her from intruding further into his private affairs."

"He stood in the rain for eight hours," I pointed out.

"That is . . . unusual," Willis, Sr., conceded.

"And what about the Heathermoor Asylum?" I asked. "It's pretty hard to ignore the ID card's implications."

"You might telephone the institution and inquire after Mr. Smith," said Willis, Sr.

I pulled Rob out of a cardboard box and into my lap. "They wouldn't release patient information to me," I said. "I don't have the necessary authority. Besides, I don't want to run the risk of alerting them to Kit's whereabouts. If he's absent without leave, they might try to round him up again."

"Quite so." Willis, Sr., tented his hands over his silk-lined waistcoat and tapped the tips of his index fingers together. "Perhaps we could ask Miss Kingsley to look into the matter."

I gaped at my father-in-law, awestruck. "William, you're a genius. I'll get right on it."

Miss Kingsley was the concierge at the Flamborough Hotel in London, and a longtime friend of the Willis family. She was discreet, efficient, and blessed with an uncanny ability to ferret out information on the most obscure individuals. If anyone could bore through a wall of institutional confidentiality, it would be the redoubtable Miss Kingsley.

"Would it be too great an imposition to request that you postpone your telephone call to Miss Kingsley until after we have dined?" said Willis, Sr. "I have fed my grandsons, but I have not yet had the opportunity to feed myself."

A wave of guilt dampened my jubilation. I'd been so preoccupied with Kit Smith that I hadn't bothered to ask how my father-in-law's day had gone, much less given a moment's thought to our evening meal.

"Dinner'll be on the table in twenty minutes," I promised, and when Willis, Sr., began to rise from his chair, I ordered him to stay put. "Relax," I said. "You've done enough for one day."

I devoted the rest of the evening to hearth and home. I whipped up a meal for Willis, Sr., bathed Will and Rob and got them off to bed, then invited my father-in-law to join me in the kitchen while I baked a double batch of angel cookies, in a belated attempt to celebrate my mother's birthday. By the time Willis, Sr., turned in for the night, it was too late to telephone Miss Kingsley.

It wasn't too late, however, to speak with Aunt Dimity. Tired though I was, I went to the study, pulled the blue journal from its niche on the bookshelves, and curled up on the tall leather armchair before the hearth.

I yipped in alarm when the journal sprang open in my hands.

It's about time. The familiar copperplate raced across the page in a nearly illegible scrawl. *I was beginning to think you'd forgotten me. Did you go to the Radcliffe? Were you allowed in to see the tramp? Have you learned anything more about him?*

"His name's Kit Smith," I began, and for the second time that evening, recounted everything I'd learned about the man in the Radcliffe Infirmary. When I'd finished, Dimity's handwriting resumed, this time at its normal pace.

I do not remember anyone called Kit Smith. Tell me again about the medals in the suede pouch.

"There's a DSO, a DFC, an Air Force Cross, and a Pathfinder badge, among others," I told her. "Why? Did you know someone who flew bombers during the war?"

In February 1943, I was given a temporary assignment with Bomber Command, at a base up in Lincolnshire. I came to know many aircrews, but none of the men with whom I worked were so highly decorated.

I slumped in the chair, discouraged. "Then we still don't know why he risked his life to come here. Julian'd say that it was just another example of Kit's crazy behavior."

Then Father Bright would be jumping to conclusions. We may not know Kit's reasons for coming to the cottage, but that doesn't mean he had none. I do wish you'd been able to see Kit more clearly. Your description of him remains woefully inadequate. Around forty years of age, tall, slender—well, he would be slender, wouldn't he, if he's suffering from malnutrition?

I bit my lip. I hadn't exactly lied to Dimity, but I hadn't told her the whole truth, either. "The cubicle was dimly lit," I said, "and Kit was wearing an oxygen mask."

And since Father Bright and the Somervilles saw Kit as you did, through a curtain of hair and beard, they wouldn't be able to describe him either. You must return to the Radcliffe after they've removed Kit's mask and take a good, long look at him. I will search my memory for anyone called Kit Smith, but I'm still counting on you to bring me an accurate description.

"I will," I promised, but as I watched Aunt Dimity's handwriting fade from the page, I wasn't sure I'd keep my promise.

I closed the blue journal and looked across the study to the desk where I'd left Kit's carryall when I'd returned from Oxford. I'd borrowed the bag from Julian, telling him, and myself, that I hadn't had time to examine its contents thoroughly, and that a closer inspection might provide a further clue to Kit's identity. I wondered now if my reasons for keeping the bag had less to do with discovering Kit's identity than with experiencing his presence.

I closed my eyes and saw Kit's face so clearly I could almost count his lashes. I saw the creases at the corners of his eyes, the sculpted cheekbones, the curving lips, and the fine, straight nose, each feature bathed and softened by golden light. Once again, those violet eyes gazed up at me and that sweet smile pierced my heart.

Why hadn't I described Kit to Aunt Dimity? Why had I withheld from her the very information she desired most? Was I afraid I might describe him all too accurately?

Suddenly, at the very edge of my hearing, I heard the distant sound of a howling wind. I trembled slightly and opened my eyes, scanning the ivy-webbed window for signs of an impending storm, but the ivy hung as still as a stenciled pattern against the glass panes. I shook my head to clear it, ran a hand through my dark crop of curls, and returned the journal to the shelves, telling myself that I was more tired than I'd thought. Kit had been caught in the blizzard, not me.

As I trudged upstairs to bed, it occurred to me that Kit's sleep might well be troubled by the memory of a howling wind. It also occurred to me that my feelings for him might not be entirely philanthropic.

9

When I saw the faint circles beneath Willis, Sr.'s clear gray eyes the next morning, I put them down to grandchild-induced battle fatigue. My sons were perfect angels, of course, but at nine months even angels could be a handful.

I had no intention of letting my father-in-law fly solo again. Once I'd finished making a few phone calls in the privacy of the study, I'd join him and the twins in the living room and resume my dual roles as mother and daughter-in-law of the year.

The first call was to Dr. Pritchard, who informed me that Kit's condition had deteriorated during the night. They'd managed to stabilize him, but he remained comatose and was now on a ventilator. The doctor concluded his report by telling me not to worry. I bit back a shout of *"How?"*, thanked him politely, and hung up the phone.

Every cell in my body wanted to dash out of the cottage and run to Kit's side, but I told myself not to be a fool. Kit was in good hands, and my presence at his bedside would make no difference to his recovery. I thought briefly of telephoning Julian Bright, then realized that he would already know of Kit's setback, since, according to Nurse Willoughby, he visited the Radcliffe every morning.

My second call was to the Willis mansion in Boston, but I was informed by the housekeeper that Bill had already left for Hyram Collier's funeral. I envisioned Mrs. Collier standing over her husband's grave, shivering in a bitter northeast wind, and was gladder than ever that Bill was there to comfort her.

My third call was to Miss Kingsley, who accepted her assignment with alacrity, promising to get back to me as soon as possible with whatever information she could glean about Kit's stay at the Heathermoor Asylum.

"Are you sure you're okay with this?" I asked. "The Flamborough must be pretty busy at this time of year."

"I could do with the distraction," Miss Kingsley told me. "If I hear 'Good King Wenceslas' one more time, I swear I'll take a gun to the roof and start picking off Salvation Army bell ringers."

"Miss Kingsley!" I gasped.

"Working in a hotel at Christmastime would be enough to drive a saint to cynicism," Miss Kingsley stated firmly. "Please tell me that your Christmas Eve party's still on. It's the only thing left to look forward to."

"It's on," I assured her, "and I'll expect you to be there, with bells on."

"No," she said, her voice shuddering. "No bells . . ."

When I finished speaking with Miss Kingsley, I picked up Kit Smith's carryall and brought it with me to the living room. I wanted to give Kit's meager belongings a second look while keeping an eye on the boys.

I should have known better. Before I got a chance to

look at anything, Will grabbed the tin mug, Rob made off with the soup spoon, and Reginald, my pink flannel rabbit, fell across the prayer book's open pages. Willis, Sr., rescued Reginald and the prayer book, then settled back in his chair to watch while I retrieved the spoon from Rob and wrested the mug from Will's grasp.

After propitiating my angels with a pair of plush elephants, I replaced everything I'd removed from the canvas bag, zipped it shut, and left it on the coffee table, vowing to wait until naptime before I made another attempt to examine its contents.

"Hmmm," said Willis, Sr. The prayer book lay open on his lap and Reg perched on the back of his chair, looking for all the world as if he were reading the book over Willis, Sr.'s shoulder. "Interesting."

"What?" I got up from the floor and went to Willis, Sr.'s side. "What's interesting?"

Willis, Sr., pointed to the top of the lefthand page. "The corner has been folded down. It may mean nothing, of course, but then again . . ."

I sat on the arm of his chair. "What's on the page?"

"Prayers for the Feast of Saint Michael and All Angels," said Willis, Sr., scanning the text. After a moment, he began reading aloud. " 'There was a war in heaven: Michael and his angels fought against the dragon. . . . And the great dragon was cast out. . . . Therefore rejoice, ye heavens, and ye that dwell in them.' " He fell silent, then began leafing through the book. He stopped when he came to a section titled *The Burial of the Dead*.

The top corner of every page in the section had been folded down.

" 'Man that is born of a woman hath but a short time to live,' " Willis, Sr., intoned, " 'and is full of misery. . . . In the midst of life we are in death. . . .' " When he turned the page, I saw that a passage had been added in tiny hand-writing between two of the prayers.

"What does it say?" I asked.

Willis, Sr., bent low over the book to read the hand-written passage. " 'The Lord is my shepherd; I shall not want. He maketh me to lie down in green pastures. . . . Yea, though I walk through the valley of the shadow of death—' "

" 'I will fear no evil, for thou art with me.' " I'd learned Psalm 23 for a drama class in high school, and it had stayed with me ever since. "Are any other corners folded down?"

Willis, Sr., closed the prayer book, then began at the beginning, inspecting each page for folded corners or minuscule handwriting, but discovered nothing more.

I took the prayer book from him and returned to the coffee table, where I gazed down at the canvas bag. " 'There was a war in heaven . . .' " I began.

" '. . . and the great dragon was cast out,' " Willis, Sr., finished.

"Prayer book . . . praying," I murmured. I had a sudden, vivid vision of Kit standing before the memorial window in the church where Anne Somerville had found him. The window's words came back to me as easily as those of the Twenty-third Psalm: " 'The people of these villages cared for the airmen. . . . They watched for them' "—I thumped the prayer book with my fist—" 'and prayed for them.' " I swung around to face Willis, Sr. "That's what Kit was doing at the airfield. He was praying for the souls of the airmen who never returned from their war with the dragon."

"Lori," Willis, Sr., said patiently, "you are theorizing in advance of the facts. We do not know if Mr. Smith marked those pages or added Psalm Twenty-three to the burial service."

I'd already picked up the telephone. "I have to call Julian," I told Willis, Sr. "I have to tell him that Kit wasn't watching for phantoms, he was praying for very real men." I dialed directory assistance, requested Saint Benedict's number, then hung up and stared at the phone, perplexed.

"Well?" said Willis, Sr. "Are you going to telephone Father Bright?"

"I can't," I said. "His phone's been disconnected." I gripped the prayer book in both hands and looked at Willis, Sr., imploringly.

"Go," he said, with a wave of his flawlessly manicured hand. "But you must promise to return by four o'clock. The rehearsal for the Nativity play begins at five."

"I won't be late." I kissed the boys, then ran to grab my shoulder bag and cashmere coat, and, as an afterthought, a tinful of angel cookies.

Saint Benedict's Hostel for Transient Men was located in a run-down redbrick building in a seedy neighborhood in East Oxford. The area was more than a bit rough. An empty lot littered with beer cans, broken glass, and discarded syringes stretched away from the side of the building, and graffiti covered the walls. It was hard to believe that such squalor could exist within hailing distance of one of the world's finest universities.

I parked the Mini directly in front of the hostel and left it with no little trepidation. As I approached Saint Benedict's front door I glanced across the empty lot, saw a small boy peering out of a broken window in a neighboring building, and thanked God that I'd brought my sons to Finch.

My timid knock was answered by a wizened little man with a green stocking cap and a distinctive body odor.

"I'm looking for Julian Bright," I said, breathing shallowly.

The little man gave me the once-over, then motioned with a clawlike hand for me to follow him. Clutching my shoulder bag tightly, I stepped into the hostel.

I felt as though I'd descended into one of the lower circles of hell. The decay besetting Saint Benedict's wasn't merely skin deep. Everywhere I looked I saw cracked plaster, water-stained walls, and peeling linoleum. An attempt had been made to keep the place tidy—the floors were swept and the windows sparkled—but it would have taken more than a broom and a squeegee to correct Saint Benedict's myriad defects.

The air was redolent of the rank aromas of boiled cabbage, damp wool, and unwashed flesh. The fug was so oppressive that it made me long for the Radcliffe's antiseptic tang, and the residents made me long for blinders. The derelicts who observed our progress as we walked down the central corridor seemed to possess every facial deformity known to man. I was so alarmed by one fellow's mashed nose and cauliflower ears that I missed my footing and nearly fell. My clumsiness won a round of guffaws from my audience and a sneer from my escort.

"You're new here," he observed in a gravelly voice.

"Brand-new," I admitted.

He gave me a jaundiced glance. "You won't last a week."

I agreed with him wholeheartedly.

After what seemed like several centuries, we reached a steamy kitchen, and Julian Bright. The priest stood at a deep double sink, scrubbing a stockpot. He wore a bibbed white apron over a black T-shirt and black jeans, and his fringe of graying hair lay in damp curls along the back of his neck.

"Lady to see you, Father," my guide announced.

Julian dried his hands on his apron as he turned to face me. "Why, Rupert, this isn't just any lady. This is the lady who saved Smitty's life."

"You saved Smitty?" Rupert's whole demeanor changed. He pulled off his green stocking cap, revealing a greasy thatch of black hair, and said gruffly, "You done good, missus. God'll bless you for it. If there's ever anything I can do for you . . ."

"You can keep an eye on her car, for a start," Julian advised.

"Will do, Father." Rupert replaced his stocking cap and headed back down the corridor.

Julian peeled off his apron and threw it on a scratched stainless-steel countertop. His T-shirt was plastered to his chest and I wondered, fleetingly, how often he worked out.

"I can't believe you're here," he said, with a warm smile.

"I tried to call, but . . ." I tore my gaze away from his finely honed pectorals and reminded myself sternly that he was a man of God and I, a happily married mother of twins. "Did you know that your phone's been disconnected?"

"Has it?" he said, in mock surprise. "No wonder His Holiness hasn't been in touch lately." He wiped the sweat from his brow. "Let's go to my office, shall we? It's less tropical than the kitchen."

Julian's office was a cramped and ill-lit oblong box overlooking the empty lot. A bank of four-drawer file cabinets occupied one side of the room; a gray steel desk, the other. On the desk sat an aged computer flanked by neatly stacked file folders, and the wall above it was covered with bus schedules, train schedules, posters, and maps. The windowsill held a spindly potted seedling pine crowned with a tinfoil star.

Julian went to the dining room to fetch a chair for me, and when he returned I saw that he'd exchanged his black T-shirt for a black turtleneck.

"Are you warm enough?" he asked, as he hung my coat on the back of the door.

"I'm fine," I said. I was wearing silk-lined pleated wool trousers and a soft, raspberry-pink lamb's wool pullover.

"The color suits you," Julian observed, eyeing my sweater. "It's very cheerful. Just what Saint Benedict's needs."

That's not all it needs, I thought, glancing up at the water-stained ceiling.

Again, Julian seemed to read my thoughts. "There's nothing glamorous about my work, Lori—no round-eyed kiddies or fluffy puppies to attract high-profile patrons. Our poster boys are toothless old men who drink too much and bathe too little. Saint Benedict is the patron saint of beggars, you know, and beggars are, as a rule, a rough lot."

"I'm sure you can handle them," I said, "and find a cure for what ails Saint Benedict's."

"Is my arrogance so obvious?" Julian said lightly.

"Your compassion is obvious," I told him.

Julian laughed, a sudden explosion of sound, harsh and mirthless. "Neither arrogance nor compassion will keep our doors open much longer. It's a miracle they haven't closed us down already."

"Who?" I asked.

"The same bureaucrats who rescinded our government funding five years ago." Julian motioned toward the files on the desk. "I've done my best to encourage private donations, but it's been an uphill battle. As I said, Saint Benedict's isn't a glamorous cause. No one wants to pose for snaps with men like Rupert."

"Why doesn't the church help out?" I asked.

"The church doesn't consider Saint Benedict's a priority," Julian replied. "It's already supporting two soup kitchens and another shelter."

"Then the men will have somewhere else to go if Saint Benedict's does close," I pointed out.

"There are other shelters," Julian agreed, "but since all of them are overcrowded and understaffed, most of my men will end up sleeping in doorways—until the police run them off. Then they'll go under bridges, into back alleys. . . . Wherever you find stray cats, you'll find my flock."

"But it's winter," I protested. "They'll freeze to death."

"It happens every day." Julian's mouth hardened briefly; then he hung his head, repentant. "Forgive me, Lori. I shouldn't speak so bluntly. I keep forgetting that you're not accustomed to such things. Apart from that . . ."

Julian's voice faded as the distant howl of a bitter wind grew louder, blanking out all other sounds. I hunched my shoulders, shuddering, and pressed a trembling hand to my forehead.

"Lori?" said Julian.

"Y-yes?" I managed, as the wind's roar faded.

"You went away." Julian peered at me closely. "Where did you go?"

"Just . . . daydreaming." I gave myself a mental shake and took the tin out of my shoulder bag. "Here. I brought you some cookies."

Julian's eyes told me that he, too, knew an evasion when he heard one, but he took the tin with evident delight. "How kind of you," he said. "I can't remember the last time anyone brought me such a treat. Is that why you came here today?"

"Yes . . . no." I took a calming breath. "I've come about Kit. I think I've figured out why he went to the airfields in

Cambridgeshire." I pulled the prayer book out of my shoulder bag and told Julian about the pages Kit had marked and the psalm he'd added to the burial service.

Julian listened intently, read through the marked pages, and finally nodded. "So . . . you believe that Kit visited abandoned bomber bases in order to hold prayer vigils for the souls of lost airmen."

"That's right," I said excitedly. "He wasn't just standing there in the rain, looking for ghosts. He was praying." When Julian said nothing, I went on. "Don't you get it? He wasn't acting on some crazy impulse. He had a reason to go to the airfields."

"It's a reason," Julian acknowledged. He leaned forward and added, very gently, "But would you call it a sane reason?"

Julian's words hit me like a body blow. I'd been eager to share my discovery with the priest, confident that he'd interpret it as I had, as yet another example of Kit's essential goodness. Instead, he'd twisted the evidence to suit his own agenda. If he had his way, Kit would spend the rest of his days cleaning the stable yard at Blackthorne Farm. A surge of fierce protectiveness brought me to my feet.

"You want to know what arrogance is?" I said. "Arrogance is thinking you know all of the answers when, in fact, you don't know a damned thing."

Julian flinched, but I wasn't finished yet.

"I think you *want* Kit to be insane," I snapped. "I think you're jealous of him because he's a better man than you. You should be ashamed of yourself, Julian Bright."

Frowning furiously, I seized my coat, stormed out of the building, and got behind the wheel of the Mini. Before I quite knew what was happening, I found myself walking through the entrance of the Radcliffe Infirmary.

10

I was halfway across the lobby when a familiar voice sang out my name.

"Lori! How are those handsome sons of yours, and where's your wanderin' husband?"

Luke Boswell came charging toward me, pushing a trolley filled with books. Luke was a middle-aged North Carolinian who'd come to Oxford on a Rhodes scholarship and never left. He owned Preacher's Antiquarian Bookstore, just off Saint Giles Road. I'd spent many hours in his shop, sipping black-currant tea and discussing his latest finds.

As Luke drew closer, his amiable expression became sober. "Your boys aren't ill, are they?"

"They're fine, Luke—and Bill is, too," I replied "Everyone's fine."

"Not everyone." Luke leaned forward, his elbows on the trolley. " 'Tis the season to be jolly, but you look mad enough to spit tacks."

"It's a long story, Luke." I noted a red plastic badge

pinned to his argyle cardigan. "I didn't know you did volunteer work here."

"I didn't, until about a month ago," Luke informed me. "A customer talked me into it, and I have to say I'm glad he did. Makes me feel like one of Santa's little old elves." He patted the trolley. "Nothin' like a good book to distract a body from what ails it."

"I hope you've thanked your customer," I said, managing a smile.

"Well, now, he's not a customer, exactly," Luke temporized. "A customer spends money, and this fellow has none to spend. He's what we used to call a *road* scholar, if you take my meanin'. Nice fellow, though. Good-hearted as the day is long. Strange, when you think that all he reads about is war."

The hairs on the back of my neck stood straight up. "What's this guy look like?"

"He's a long, tall drink of water," Luke answered. "Wild hair, big old beard, dressed on the shabby side. Hasn't been in for a few days, but I expect he'll be back."

The hospital lobby seemed to spin around me. "Does he have a name?"

"Kit," Luke replied. "Kit Smith. But he says some folk call him Smitty. Why do you ask?"

I motioned toward the trolley. "Are you finished here, Luke? Are you heading back to the shop?"

"Soon as I fetch my coat," he replied. "Why?"

"I'm coming with you," I said. "I'll explain why on the way."

We walked to Preacher's, fighting our way down Saint Giles Road through a swarming stream of shoppers caught up in the holiday frenzy. Most looked haggard, some merely anxious; a rare few smiled contentedly. As I walked along, telling Luke about Kit, I was jostled by jutting elbows, bumped by bulging shopping bags, and assaulted by the tinny strains of competing carols that spilled into the street each time a shop door opened. By the time we reached Preacher's Lane, I was ready to strangle Father Christmas.

As we turned into the lane, I caught sight of two rheumy-eyed men crouched in a doorway, as though they'd been shunted to a side inlet by the rushing tide of shoppers on Saint Giles. They were unshaven, filthy, and sharing a bottle between them. I averted my eyes from the pathetic scene, but it was to no avail.

"Give us a kiss, lady!" roared one.

"Give us a tenner and I'll let you kiss my arse!" called the other.

The pair laughed uproariously.

Luke seized my arm and hustled me along, muttering, "They're not all like Kit."

"They certainly aren't," I agreed.

We said nothing more until we reached the bookstore.

"Kit told me they wouldn't let him into the college libraries on account of his appearance," Luke said, hanging our coats behind the front counter. "Now there's high-class idiocy for you. Any fool could see that he's bright as a button. Said his daddy used to give lectures at the university."

"Did you think he was telling the truth?" I asked.

Luke shrugged. "He might've thought I needed an excuse to let him read my books gratis, but I didn't. I don't care what folk look like. Hell, half the students comin' through here dress worse'n old Kit."

I nodded. "Did he say anything else about his family?"

Luke shook his head. "Not much of a talker, truth to tell. Preferred reading. Come on, I'll show you what he read."

Luke led me through the narrow aisles to an alcove labeled MILITARY HISTORY. I gazed at the floor-to-ceiling shelves in dismay.

"Did he read everything?" I asked.

"Nothing but the books on Bomber Command." Luke began selecting volumes from the crowded shelves. "Let's see if he marked my books the same way he marked that prayer book of his."

Luke and I spent the next two hours examining two dozen books, but we found no folded corners, no annotations, nothing to indicate a special interest in a particular page or passage. When we finished, I took up a general history of Bomber Command and asked Luke if I could borrow it.

As he wrapped the volume in brown paper, the string of bells on the front door jingled and a shambling figure wearing a green stocking cap sidled into the shop, wafting his distinctive body odor before him.

"Rupert?" I said, my nose wrinkling involuntarily.

"That's right, missus. Me mates told me you'd be here." The little man was dressed in multiple layers of grubby vests and sweaters topped with an oversized raincoat. "Got something for you."

"Really?" I seriously doubted that such a shabby character could have anything I'd want. "What's that?"

Rupert reached inside his raincoat and produced a thick scroll of paper. It was charred at one end, as though it had been thrust into a fire and hastily removed. "Smitty left it to be burnt with the rest of the rubbish at Saint B's, but I got it back for him. Didn't seem right to burn it, not after he took such trouble over it."

I took the charred scroll from him hesitantly. "Why didn't you give it to Father Bright?"

"He's got a mortal load on his back, does Father Bright, what with keeping Saint B's ticking and all," Rupert replied. "Didn't want to give him something else to worry about." He motioned toward the scroll. "You'll give it back to Smitty when he's fit again, will you?"

"I will," I promised, and reached into my shoulder bag. "Let me give you something for your troubles."

"I done it for Smitty, missus," he said. "I don't want no reward."

"A cup of tea, at least," offered Luke.

"Ta, but I got to get back to Saint B's. Father Bright'll try to do it all himself if I'm not there to get the crew cracking. Cheers, missus." The little man pulled his stocking cap snugly over his ears and shuffled out of the shop.

"Looks like you're makin' all kinds of new friends," Luke commented. "Let's see what old Rupert turned up."

The scroll was made up of some two hundred sheets of onionskin, each thin sheet covered with hundreds of names written in the same minute script Willis, Sr., had discovered in the prayer book. An abbreviated military rank proceeded each name.

"Flyin' Officer A. R. Layton," Luke read aloud, squinting at the tiny writing. "Leadin' Aircraftman L. J. Turek. Looks like they're all flyboys, Lori. A roll call of the dead."

"The dead?" I said, fingering the thick scroll. "There must be thousands of names listed here. That's an awfully high casualty rate."

"Bomber Command lost round about sixty thousand men, give or take a few," Luke informed me. "They took a hard hit."

As Luke wrapped the charred scroll in another sheet of brown paper, I felt as confused as Rupert. Why would Kit attempt to destroy a list of names so painstakingly compiled? Why compile the list in the first place? If he was praying for the dead, wouldn't a general prayer suffice?

"You sure have taken an interest in old Kit," Luke observed, handing the scroll to me.

"I guess I feel responsible for him," I mumbled. "He collapsed in my driveway, after all."

Luke looked at me from beneath his bushy eyebrows. "The Somervilles aren't offerin' him such a bad deal, Lori. I'm not sayin' Kit's dangerous-crazy, but from what you've told me, he does seem a mite peculiar."

Luke must have seen a tack-spitting gleam in my eyes, because he immediately changed the subject. "Lookin' forward to the Christmas Eve party. Got my red suspenders starched special for the occasion."

I smiled briefly, thanked him for the loan of the book, and left the shop.

As I made my way up Preacher's Lane, I heard a shout from the pair of winos I'd seen earlier. I pulled my coat collar up and prepared to hurry on, but something made me glance in their direction.

The two ragged men stood at attention, their hands raised to the brims of their cloth caps in a shaky salute. Rupert's mates, I thought, and wondered if they were ex-airmen as well. I acknowledged their gesture with an awkward bob of the head, then hurriedly retraced my steps to the Radcliffe.

I stood outside Kit's cubicle, my palms pressed to the glass, watching his chest rise and fall in the unnaturally regular rhythm induced by the ventilator. I couldn't approach his bedside—visitors had been barred ever since he'd had his setback—so I spoke to him silently, sending my thoughts through the glass barrier, telling him that I would do everything in my power to keep him from being held captive by his well-intentioned friends.

"Miss Shepherd?"

The sound of Nurse Willoughby's voice made me jump.

"Sorry to startle you," said the young red-haired nurse. "I was wondering if you'd do me a favor."

"Of course," I said.

"There was a woman here earlier today, a friend of Mr. Smith's—"

"Anne Somerville?" I put in.

"That's right. She brought something for Mr. Smith. She thought it might comfort him, but . . . well, it looks rather nasty to me. I was wondering if you'd take it away."

Nurse Willoughby held out her hand and I took a quick step backward.

"Is it dead?" I said suspiciously, eyeing the object in her hand.

"It's a toy," she corrected. She held the stuffed animal up at eye level. "A horse, I think."

I took the battered plaything from her. The little brown horse with the black mane and tail had been loved nearly to pieces. The seam in his belly had been resewn with red thread, his hide was patched in three places, and the black yarn of his mane was hopelessly tangled. As he flopped in my hands, his legs splayed, his nose touching my palm, I felt my heart melt. It must have cost Anne Somerville dearly to leave such a cherished companion behind.

Nurse Willoughby patted his head apologetically. "We can't keep him here, I'm afraid. He's positively virulent."

"I'll take care of him," I assured her. I tucked the brown horse into my shoulder bag and turned once again to gaze at Kit. Did he know how many people cared about him? I wondered: Did he know how many hearts he'd touched?

Slowly, reluctantly, I turned away and headed for home, hoping that a message from Miss Kingsley awaited me.

I stopped by Anscombe Manor on the way home, to have a word with Emma Harris. Emma knew everything there was to know about two subjects: gardening and computers. I was hoping her computer skills would help me dig up information on the names listed in the charred scroll.

I found her in the great hall, a half-timbered banquet room Derek had just finished restoring. She was hanging evergreen swags from the massive rafters when I entered the hall, but put down her hammer and descended the ladder when she saw me.

"No Peter again this Christmas," she announced, pulling a wry face. "Derek had high hopes of seeing his peripatetic son this year, but it's the one gift I can't give him."

"Is Peter still up the Amazon?" I asked.

"With a paddle, one hopes." Emma beckoned to me to join her at the long trestle table in the center of the hall. The table was piled with ornaments and lights, packets of tinsel and boxes of candles. "All systems are go for the Christmas Eve party here. Let's make sure I've got it right: The festivities will kick off around noon at your place. Everyone will go from there to the schoolhouse to see the Nativity play, then come here for the rest of the evening. Is that the plan?"

"That's the plan," I said. "And again, thanks hugely for putting up my out-of-town guests."

"I'm glad to do it. It'll help take Derek's mind off of

Peter." She offered her hammer to me. "Haven't come to lend a hand by any chance, have you?"

"Just the opposite," I said sheepishly. "I've come to ask for your help yet again." I took the scroll out of my shoulder bag, stripped away the brown paper, and carefully peeled off the outermost sheet of onionskin. "Would you check out some of the names listed here? I need to know if they belong to men who were killed while serving with Bomber Command in World War Two."

Emma took the sheet from me and examined the tiny handwriting. "I'll get on to the Imperial War Museum," she said. "Someone there should be able to check the records for me." She shook her head, giving me a dubious look. "It's a strange subject to be researching at Christmastime. Where'd the list come from?"

"Come over for a cup of tea and I'll tell you all about it," I offered. "Right now I have to get home and feed William. He's got a rehearsal tonight."

"Give him my condolences," Emma said, with a laugh. "Nice coat, by the way. And I covet those boots."

I brushed aside the compliments, feeling vaguely guilty about the amount of money I'd spent on my winter wardrobe. "They're warm," I allowed.

"They're gorgeous," Emma retorted. She held up the scroll. "I can't guarantee speedy delivery. I've got an awful lot on my plate."

"Most of which I piled there," I acknowledged. "Just do the best you can and I'll be even deeper in your debt."

It was dark by the time I reached the cottage, so it wasn't until I'd pulled into the graveled drive that I saw the parked Land Rover.

"Saint Christopher?" I said, bewildered. I shut off the engine and hurried inside, going straight to the living room without bothering to take off my coat.

Julian Bright sat in Bill's favorite armchair, with Will in the crook of his arm, chatting easily with Willis, Sr. When he saw me, he jumped to his feet.

"Hello." His smile was tentative, as if he was unsure of his welcome.

"Hi," I replied.

Julian shifted Will from one arm to the other. "May I speak with you?"

"Sure." I glanced self-consciously at Willis, Sr., then jutted my chin toward the front door. "It's not too bad out. Let's take a walk."

Julian handed Will to Willis, Sr., and followed me into the hall. He grabbed his black leather jacket from the coat rack and slipped it on as we stepped outside.

The air was crisp, the sky vibrant with stars, and the snow crunched underfoot as we walked down the flagstone path. Julian hunched his shoulders against the chilly breeze and tucked his hands deep into his jacket pockets, but when I slipped on an icy patch, he reached out quick as lightning and caught my arm. He kept hold of my arm as he stepped in front of me.

"I'm sorry," he said.

His hand was warm and strong. My breath came raggedly, showing white against his jacket as I recalled, with alarming clarity, the compact muscles beneath the supple leather. My heart gave a disturbing flutter and I quickly averted my gaze, saying, "I'm the one who should apologize."

"No." Julian released my arm and stood back to survey the cottage. His brown eyes glittered in the light from the bow windows as his gaze traveled up the mellow stone walls to the snow-covered slate roof. "It's enchanting . . . like something out of a fairy tale. How can you bear to leave? If it were mine, I'd close the doors behind me and never come out again."

"No, you wouldn't," I chided. "You'd turn it into a cottage hospital or a refuge for unwed mothers."

"Unwed mothers don't need refuges anymore." Julian turned his face toward me. "Show me where you found him."

We crossed the graveled drive and stood before the lilac bushes, gazing at the packed snow that marked the spot where Kit had lain. I showed Julian where Bill had knelt to check Kit's pulse, and where I'd bent to lift Kit's legs as we'd carried him into the cottage. I didn't mention the shudder of revulsion that had passed through me at the thought of touching Kit's ragged trousers.

Julian listened without comment, then walked with me up the graveled drive to the bridle path. The stars were bright enough to light our way, and Nell's sleigh had left a trail of tamped snow for us to follow. We walked in silence, save for the crunch of snow beneath our boots and the creak of branches in the rising wind. It wasn't until we'd rounded a bend and the lights from the cottage had vanished behind us that Julian spoke.

"I've examined my conscience," he said, "and discovered an element of truth in what you said to me at Saint Benedict's."

"The last time I looked, arrogance wasn't a mortal sin," I told him.

"Not the arrogance," said Julian. "The jealousy." He paused to gaze up at the stars. "Do you remember asking me about my clerical collar?"

I thought back to our conversation in the Land Rover,

on the way to Blackthorne Farm. "I asked if you'd taken it off to avoid unnecessary confrontations."

"And I gave an unsatisfactory reply." Julian scuffed at the snow with the toe of his black leather boot. "The truth isn't easy for me to admit. I told myself at the time that I did it to become a better priest, but I know now that my decision had more to do with ego than vocation." He shuddered slightly as an icy gust rattled the trees. "I've worked hard to keep Saint Benedict's open, Lori, to keep a roof over the men's heads and food in their bellies. Yet my flock, for the most part, treats me as nothing more than a well-meaning bureaucrat.

"They treated Kit as a pastor. From the moment he arrived, they confided in him, asked his advice, and left me to carry on with the paperwork." Julian fixed his gaze on the snowy path. "I envied his rapport with the men. I thought removing my collar would make it easier for them to approach me, but it wasn't about *clothing*. It was about *grace*. Envy blinded me to the very quality that drew the men to Kit. Where there was goodness, I chose to see madness." Julian let out his breath, like a pricked balloon. "What would I do if Christ walked into my hostel, Lori? Would I envy him? Would I think him mad?"

"You'd put a roof over his head and food in his belly," I said softly. "Those aren't small things." I hesitated, then slipped my arm through his. "It's no use trying to be perfect, Julian. Sometimes we have to settle for being good enough."

He peered down at me anxiously. "But am I? Am I good enough?"

I laughed in disbelief. "I wish you could see yourself walking through the Radcliffe. You can't go ten steps without someone calling out to you. They love you there, and they need you. Just like the men at Saint Benedict's."

"Whom I've failed," Julian said.

"It's not your failure," I declared. "You're doing your best by those men, and anyone who does his best is good enough for me. God's lucky to have you on her side."

Julian's slow smile was as beautiful as the star-filled sky. "She is, is she?"

"She certainly is," I said brusquely. "Now stop feeling sorry for yourself, Julian Bright, and help me help Kit."

He stood to attention. "What can I do?"

I told him about Miss Kingsley's assignment to look into Kit's stay at the Heathermoor Asylum, Luke Boswell's acquaintance with Kit, and Rupert's unexpected gift. I was particularly careful to explain why Rupert had given the scroll to me instead of to Julian.

"Doesn't want to add to my burdens, eh?" Julian shook his head. "I'll have to speak with Rupert about that."

"Don't you dare," I threatened. "Rupert enjoys looking after you. Let him."

Julian conceded the point, then returned to the subject of the scroll. "A roll call of the dead to go with the service for the burial of the dead," he said. "You may be right after all, Lori. It seems that Kit was holding private prayer vigils at the bomber bases in Cambridgeshire. But why?"

I raised my hands, palms toward the sky. "There has to be a personal connection. Maybe his father served with Bomber Command and made a deathbed wish that his son go out and pray for his fellow airmen. We'll know more after Emma checks out some of the names."

"Kit's father . . ." Julian stroked his goatee thoughtfully. "If he really did lecture at one of the colleges, someone might remember him. I'll ask around."

"How?" I asked. "We don't know his name."

"I'll try Christopher Smith," said Julian. "Kit's a diminutive of Christopher, and fathers have been known to name sons after themselves."

"Sounds good," I said. "There's one other thing I'd like you to do."

"Name it," said Julian.

"Telephone your contacts in the refuge network," I said. "Find out if Kit stayed in other shelters. If we can reconstruct his movements, we may be able to figure out where he came from originally."

"And perhaps find his family." Julian blew on his cupped palms and rubbed his hands together. "Might be a bit tricky, though, the telephoning."

I slapped my forehead. "I forgot. Your phone's been disconnected." I reached into my coat pocket and pulled out my cellular phone. "Here, use mine."

"I couldn't," Julian protested. "It's far too expensive."

I thrust the cell phone into his hands. "It's for Kit's sake, remember? And don't worry about the expense. I've got tons of—" I broke off as an awful thought intruded. "What time is it?"

Julian checked his watch. "A quarter to five."

"Oh my Go"—I caught myself—"gosh! We have to get back right away." I grabbed Julian's arm and hurried him up the bridle path, kicking myself for forgetting about Willis, Sr.'s rehearsal.

Willis, Sr., had his coat in hand when we came bursting through the front door of the cottage. I gasped out an apology, which he accepted gracefully, but it wasn't until he'd driven off in the Mercedes that I thought to ask if he'd had dinner.

"I am the worst daughter-in-law who ever lived," I said mournfully, watching the Mercedes's taillights through the bow windows.

"I wouldn't say that." Julian came up behind me and put a comforting hand on my shoulder. "I'd say you're good enough."

I sent Julian off with the rest of the angel cookies to share with the men at Saint Benedict's. When he'd gone, it was playtime, bathtime, and finally, bedtime for the twins.

After clearing the kitchen, straightening the living room, and mopping up the bathroom, I was too worn out to even consider decorating the cottage. Instead, I carried Kit's canvas carryall upstairs to the master bedroom, placing it on the blanket chest at the foot of the bed, where the boys were less likely to get at it. As I tucked the brown horse in beside the suede pouch, I wondered for the thousandth time what had brought Kit to a honey-colored cottage in the Cotswolds, in the midst of a winter storm.

With an ear attuned to the telephone, and Miss Kingsley's much-anticipated call, I tore the wrapping paper from the book Luke had loaned me, scanned the table of contents, and saw a chapter title that caught my interest: "The Birth of the Pathfinder Force." Intrigued, I sat on the edge of the bed and started reading.

Two hours later, I heard a sneeze and glanced up from my book to see Willis, Sr., standing in the doorway.

"I have looked in on my grandsons," he informed me, "and now I shall retire for the night."

"Let me get you a bite to eat," I insisted, rising hastily from the bed.

"I am not excessively hungry." Willis, Sr., touched a linen handkerchief to his patrician nose. "Did you learn anything of value in Oxford today?"

I needed no further encouragement to tell him everything I'd learned about the mysterious, charismatic man known as Kit Smith.

I repeated the story to Bill three hours later, when he telephoned from Boston. Willis, Sr., had gone to bed and the boys were sleeping soundly in the nursery. I'd been lying on the bed in the master bedroom for some time, fully clothed and staring at the ceiling, when Bill called.

"You've taken a surprising interest in this Kit Smith," Bill observed, echoing Luke Boswell's words.

"Wouldn't you?" I retorted. "He's either a madman or a saint."

"You seem to be leaning toward the latter," said Bill.

"Someone has to," I said. "Practically everyone else thinks he's nuts."

There was a pause. Then Bill said carefully, "What if they're right?"

I stiffened and thought, *Et tu,* Bill? "They're not," I said shortly. "What time is your plane arriving tomorrow?"

Bill cleared his throat. "To tell you the truth, that's why I called. . . ."

I listened calmly while Bill explained why he wouldn't be coming home on Friday. Hyram Collier's widow, it seemed, needed help settling her late husband's estate, and Bill felt duty-bound to offer his services. I gave my blessing to his extended stay. How could I object to him helping an old friend's widow in her time of need?

"I don't care how long you're away," I told him, "as long as you're home by Christmas Eve."

"I'll be home long before then," Bill promised.

I hung up the phone, turned off the bedside lamp, and lay back against the pillows. I'd intended to speak with

Aunt Dimity before turning in, but the long day had finally caught up with me. All I wanted was a hot bath, a flannel nightie, and sleep.

Moonlight streamed into the bedroom, casting long-fingered shadows across the ceiling. The shadows bucked and quivered as a biting northeast wind shook the leafless trees beyond the windowpane. I trailed my fingers across Bill's pillow, thought of Kit's exquisite hands, then crawled to the foot of the bed to kneel before the canvas carryall.

It seemed strangely alive in the trembling moonlight, like the crumpled body of a man struggling for breath. I touched a fingertip to a roughened seam, then slowly un-zipped the zipper and slipped a hand inside. The suede pouch full of medals clinked softly as I pressed it to my lips.

"Kit," I whispered, "why did you come here?"

11

Both Willis, Sr., and I were in pensive moods at breakfast the following morning. When I asked how the rehearsal had gone, he gave a forlorn little sigh and set his toast aside, untasted.

"It's an amateur production," I reminded him.

"Of that there can be no doubt whatsoever," he declared. "The shepherds can scarcely hobble across the stage, the three wise men are being played by women, the angel of the Lord must perch precariously atop an unstable stepladder, and as for Eleanor . . ." He clucked his tongue sadly.

I paused with a last bite of toast halfway to my mouth. Willis, Sr., was usually full of praise for Nell Harris. I'd expected him to enjoy playing Joseph opposite her Mary. "What's wrong with Nell?"

"Some of her ideas will have to be revised," said Willis, Sr. "I do realize that her character is supposed to be with child, but I cannot recall a single scriptural passage describing the Holy Virgin as suffering from morning sickness."

"Morning sickness?" I repeated.

"*Violent* morning sickness," Willis, Sr., said darkly. "Nor do I recall the Virgin toppling from her donkey in a dead faint. I was most surprised when Eleanor landed at my feet."

"I bet she was, too." I popped the toast into my mouth and began clearing the table, taking care to step around the twins and over an assortment of pots and pans—their second-favorite toys—on my way to the sink.

"Mrs. Bunting said nothing to me about catching a fainting virgin," Willis, Sr., pointed out, "but then, Mrs. Bunting scarcely spoke all evening. She may be the play's nominal director, but Mrs. Kitchen is clearly in command." He pushed his omelet away, uneaten. "A most unfortunate turn of events, in my opinion."

"Did Peggy give you a hard time?" I asked, knowing full well that Peggy Kitchen was constitutionally incapable of doing anything else.

"Mrs. Kitchen took issue with my American accent," said Willis, Sr., indignantly. "When I ventured to point out that the play's events took place nearly two thousand years ago in the Middle East and that all of our accents were therefore suspect, she told me in no uncertain terms that Joseph would speak the Queen's English or none at all."

I winced. As a lawyer, my father-in-law took great pride in his elocutionary skills. Peggy Kitchen had hit him where it hurt. "What did Lilian say to that?"

"Mrs. Bunting covered her face with her hands and retreated to the cloakroom," said Willis, Sr., "where she remained for the duration of the evening. I must say that I was tempted to join her."

I surveyed his resigned expression and felt a pang of conscience. He'd done me a big favor by filling in for Bill. I had to think of a way to cheer him up.

"Look," I said, leaning back against the sink, "why don't you and I corral the boys in the playpen and get to work decorating the cottage? It'll take your mind off of Peggy Kitchen and be a nice surprise for Bill when he gets home."

Willis, Sr., shook his head. "It is an enticing suggestion, Lori, but I must confess that I do not feel up to it." He touched his forehead with the back of his hand. "I seem to be unusually warm, in fact. I believe I may have caught the vicar's cold."

It wasn't until he spoke those words that I noticed his heightened color and a mild hoarseness in his mellow voice. Guilt stabbed me with a thousand sharpened blades. For the past three days I'd been so absorbed in Kit Smith that Willis, Sr., could have dropped dead at my feet without attracting my attention. It wasn't good enough, not by a long shot, no matter what Julian said.

I immediately ordered Willis, Sr., into his silk pajamas, tucked him up in the master bedroom, and brought tea to him on a tray. While he sipped languidly, I called Dr. Finisterre, the semiretired physician who ministered to the local population.

The doctor arrived at the cottage a half hour later. I led him to the master bedroom, then paced the hallway, wringing my hands. My father-in-law had a heart condition. If his cold turned into pneumonia, he might end up in intensive care, like Kit, with IVs in his arms, and a bank of beeping monitors looming over him. *And it would be my fault.* By the time Dr. Finisterre emerged from the master bedroom, I was nearly in tears.

"His heart?" I said anxiously.

"Nothing to do with his heart," the doctor said. "Your

father-in-law has a head cold. It's par for the course, this
time of year. No need to call out the RAF." He gave a rum-
bling chuckle as he descended the stairs. "I should keep
him away from the twins for the time being. It's for his
benefit, not theirs. William needs rest."

I let out a sobbing sigh and covered my mouth with my
hand.

"Get hold of yourself, Lori," Dr. Finisterre scolded.
"No need to make such a fuss over a simple head cold." He
pulled on his black wool coat, placed his homburg on his
head, and opened the front door. "Bed rest, fluids, and as-
pirin will do the trick. William'll be right as rain in a few
days."

I thanked the doctor fervently, closed the door behind
him, and leaned against it, weak-kneed with relief. From
now on, I vowed, Kit Smith would take a backseat to my
family. As I went upstairs to check on Willis, Sr., however,
one part of my mind was still attuned to the telephone and
the sound of Miss Kingsley's voice.

I was in the kitchen the next day, laboring over a vat of
homemade chicken soup and wondering why Miss Kingsley hadn't called, when the March of the Widows began.
I'd known that widows made up a large segment of Finch's
modest population, but I'd had no idea how large a segment until the eligible male in my master bedroom began
sneezing. It was as if he'd issued a mating call.

The cottage was besieged by a chattering mob of white-
haired dears bearing bits of flannel ("to tuck about his poor
weak chest"), bowls of blancmange ("so soothing to a
scratchy throat"), embroidered sleeping caps, crocheted
foot-warmers, and several months' worth of casseroles. I
felt as though I were holding a wake.

A wake might have been in order had I fed my ailing swain the curious nostrums offered by his aged groupies. Bottles filled with glutinous brown liquids and jars of hideous gray jellies were offered with exact directions for their use. I baked another batch of angel cookies to give as thank-you's to each amateur physician but flushed their malodorous concoctions down the toilet.

The only home remedy I would countenance was the tea Emma Harris brought over from Anscombe Manor on Saturday afternoon. If Emma said that burdock-root tea would ease Willis, Sr.'s chest congestion, I believed her.

I invited Emma to stay for a cup of nonmedicinal tea, and after looking in on my patient and putting the boys down for their naps, I joined her in the living room, where she was surveying my raftered ceiling and oak mantelpiece with a puzzled frown.

"Looks like the Christmas fairy's passed you by," she commented as she settled beside me on the couch. "What happened to all of the holly you gathered, and the evergreen boughs? Shouldn't they be up by now?"

"Yep," I acknowledged, filling her cup. "Bill and I were on the verge of decorating when he was called away to attend a funeral in Boston. I thought I might tackle the job with William's help, but then he caught his cold."

"So what have you been up to?" Emma raised her teacup to her lips and took a sip.

"I've been lusting after a comatose stranger and a Roman Catholic priest," I tossed off nonchalantly. "You?"

Emma choked and sputtered, splashing tea down the front of her handknit heather-gray sweater. I quickly took the teacup from her hand and dabbed at her sweater with a calico napkin.

"F-forget about the sweater," Emma managed, waving off my ministrations. "T-tell me about the priest!"

So I told her about Julian, about his self-doubt, dedication, and touching vulnerability, and I told her about Kit, who still lay unconscious in intensive care. By the time I finished, Emma's sweater had dried and the tea had grown cold.

"Now I understand what Peggy Kitchen was grumbling about." Emma kicked off her shoes, curled her legs beneath her, and turned to face me. "When I went into the Emporium this morning she muttered something about you flooding the village with undesirables. I thought she was talking about your Christmas Eve party, but she must have meant Kit." Emma giggled wickedly. "Too bad Julian doesn't wear his collar. That would really give Peggy something to talk about."

"Papists and vagrants." I clasped my hands over my heart. "*My people.* But seriously, Emma"—I put my feet on the coffee table and rested my head on the back of the couch—"I don't know why I feel so strongly about these two men."

"Well, you've teamed up with Julian, haven't you? Being part of a team can make you feel very close to someone. As far as Kit's concerned . . ." Emma reached for Reginald, who'd somehow ended up between the sofa cushions. "I think you want to mother him. It's only natural. After all, he's even more helpless than your babies."

I pursed my lips, marveling at Emma's ability to drain the passion from the most emotionally charged situations. "In other words," I said dryly, "I'm seething with a combination of team spirit and maternal instinct?"

"I wouldn't rule out lust," Emma temporized. "You do have a weak spot for wounded princes." She gave me a sly, sidelong glance. "I'd better tell Bill to walk with a limp when he gets home."

"If he's not home by Christmas Eve," I growled, "I'll give him a limp."

"See?" said Emma. "You're still in love with your husband." She propped Reginald on the arm of the couch and folded her arms. "I ran a search on a random sample of names from Kit's scroll yesterday. Three of the men were killed in action, flying bombers over Germany. One was a POW. The rest survived the war without a scratch."

"The living and the dead," I murmured pensively. "It's not what I expected."

"Kit squeezed in about six hundred names per page," Emma explained. "That's over a hundred thousand names. The man at the Imperial War Museum put the total number of men who served with Bomber Command at one hundred twenty-five thousand. It looks as if Kit listed them all."

"I suppose the living need prayers as much as the dead," I reasoned.

"Maybe more so," said Emma. "May I have a look at those medals Kit was carrying?"

"Of course." While I fetched the suede pouch from the master bedroom, Emma took a pen and notebook from her purse. When I returned, she made a complete inventory of the pouch's contents, listing every badge, medal, ribbon, and bar.

"What are you up to?" I asked.

"It seems to me," she said, tucking the notebook back into her purse, "that only a handful of men would have been so highly decorated during the war. If I put the list of medals out on the Internet, maybe someone will recognize it and tell us who they belong to. Assuming they all belong to one man."

"It's worth a try," I said. Emma started to get up, but I

put a hand on her arm to restrain her. "Emma, my best and dearest friend," I said, in my most wheedling tones, "would you please do another favor for me?"

Emma eyed me suspiciously. "Depends on what it is."

"I promised William that I'd stand in for him at tonight's rehearsal," I informed her. "And I was hoping you'd be an absolute angel and babysit for me. It'll just be for a couple of hours, and I'll have the boys bathed and in their pajamas by the time you get here."

"You want *me* to look after the twins?" Emma gaped in disbelief. Emma's stepchildren had come to her fully weaned and potty-trained. She claimed to have no discernible maternal instinct.

"Either that or spend the evening in Finch with Peggy Kitchen," I said, fluttering my eyelashes.

"I'd *love* to look after the twins," Emma declared. "If things get too desperate, Derek can always bail me out."

I heaved a sigh of relief and gave her a hug. Emma's husband knew all there was to know about babies. With Derek as backup, Emma would have a peaceful, trouble-free evening.

I somehow doubted that the same would hold true for me.

12

Finch sparkled like a cheap dime-store bracelet that evening. Each building on the square had been outlined in fairy lights, in imitation of the annual display at Harrods, and garish garlands had been wound around each tree. The pub's plastic choirboys swayed drunkenly in the icy breeze and Sally Pyne's Santa heads leered from the tearoom's shadowy windows. The darkness softened the features of Peggy Kitchen's mad-eyed, mechanical Father Christmas, however, and made him appear marginally less hostile.

Every business on the square seemed to be closed for the evening, but the schoolhouse had come alive. Light shone from the gothic windows, and smoke rose from the narrow chimney. The succession of frigid days following the blizzard had left a glaze of ice across the schoolyard, but the show was going on regardless, thanks to a thick layer of sand spread across the treacherous surface by Mr. Barlow. The retired mechanic stood in the doorway admiring his handiwork, and Buster, his yappy terrier, barked a greeting as I approached.

I bent to scratch Buster's chin, then straightened and cocked an ear toward the sound of voices coming from within the schoolhouse. "I guess everyone's shut up shop to come to the rehearsal, huh?"

"You guess right," Mr. Barlow answered, ushering me into the cloakroom. "Won't be a business open in Finch from now until the ruddy thing's done with." He set his sand bucket on a wooden stool and closed the door behind us. "William feeling better, I hope? And how's that chap you found in your driveway? Hasn't packed it in, has he?"

I thanked Mr. Barlow for his interest and gave him a general health report: Willis, Sr., had stopped sneezing, but another day or two in bed wouldn't do him any harm; Kit Smith remained unconscious.

"Poor chap." Mr. Barlow shook his head, then motioned toward the former classroom that now served as an all-purpose meetingplace. "Best get inside and do your bit. If you ask me, Mrs. Bunting's in over her head. She's got Sally Pyne, Christine Peacock, and Peggy Kitchen playing the three wise men—in false beards!"

"She didn't have much luck finding male volunteers," I reminded him. "Are you in the play?"

"I'm on lights," Mr. Barlow stated flatly. "You wouldn't catch me parading—" He broke off abruptly and colored to his roots. "Not that there's anything wrong with it, mind. I'm sure we're all grateful to William for pitching in."

"Who's playing Herod?" I asked, easing him off the hook.

"Jasper Taxman," Mr. Barlow replied, grinning broadly. "Don't know what Mrs. Bunting was thinking."

Nor did I. It would be difficult to find a more self-effacing man than Jasper Taxman. The audience would have to summon up a superhuman suspension of disbelief to accept him as a paranoid megalomaniac plotting a search-and-destroy mission against a newborn.

"Able Farnham and George Wetherhead'll do as the shepherds," Mr. Barlow allowed, "so long as they don't have to move."

I nodded my understanding. An old hip injury forced George Wetherhead to walk with the aid of a three-pronged cane, and ancient Mr. Farnham was so frail that he could scarcely cross the square without toppling over. I trembled to think what might happen if either man got too close to the edge of the stage.

"And then there's Miranda Morrow," Mr. Barlow said thoughtfully. "She's a comely lass, no doubt about it, but I'm not convinced she's right for the angel of the Lord."

"Miranda Morrow's playing the angel of the Lord?" I said, astonished. Since Miranda Morrow was Finch's resident witch and a practicing pagan, her casting gave new meaning to the word "ecumenical."

"She was the only one willing to make the wings," Mr. Barlow explained. "Best get inside," he added, nodding toward the schoolroom. "They'll be getting under way soon."

I gave Buster's ears a cuddle, passed through the cloakroom, and entered the schoolhouse proper.

An impressive amount of work had already been done to turn the room into a serviceable theater. Folding chairs were piled to one side of the room, ready to be deployed on the big night; a stage had been erected over the dais which had once held the schoolmaster's desk; and heavy green drapes cut off the far corners of the room, creating what I assumed to be men's and women's dressing areas.

The noise level was close to deafening as cast and crew went about their assorted tasks. Sally Pyne hunched over her sewing machine, Christine and Dick Peacock dis-

pensed tea from a massive urn, and Jasper Taxman, Peggy
Kitchen's erstwhile fiancé, knelt beside a canvas flat, painting scenes allegedly depicting the Holy Land. Mr. Taxman's eye for color was all that one would expect from
a retired accountant: the hills surrounding Bethlehem
were a lurid shade of green reminiscent of a badly cleaned
aquarium.

Peggy Kitchen stood over Mr. Taxman, offering helpful
advice. Finch's undisputed empress had cloaked her ma-
ture figure in a remarkable red velvet garment that would
have suggested a burnoose more convincingly had she remembered to remove the drapery rings from the hem.
Her head was crowned with a spangled turban straight
out of a 1940s melodrama, and the lower half of her face
was covered by a woolly black false beard. The exotic effect was heightened by her trademark rhinestone-studded
eyeglasses.

Burt Hodge, a local farmer, knelt in front of the stage,
hammering on an oversized manger, while his wife sat
nearby, nursing Piero, their four-month-old son. Piero
had been awarded the coveted role of Our Lord and Savior
by virtue of the fact that he was still too young to climb out
of the manger.

Lilian Bunting sat on a folding chair midway down the
room, with a pencil in her hand and an open script
perched on her knee. Nell Harris was nowhere in sight,
but Bertie, her chocolate-brown teddy bear, sat on a chair
beside Lilian's, dressed in a black beret, a white turtleneck, and tiny jodhpurs, a diminutive assistant director.

Lilian looked up as Nell emerged from behind the green
drapes at the front of the schoolroom. Nell's golden curls
gleamed like an aureole around her flawless oval face,
and her costume was superb—an unadorned white shift
beneath the blue velvet cape she'd worn when she'd come

to the cottage in her sleigh. She looked innocent, vulnerable, ethereally beautiful—and about thirteen months pregnant.

"Lady Eleanor," Lilian said meekly, "what have you got under your shift?"

Nell placed her hands on her bulging abdomen. "A bolster."

"Kindly replace it with a smaller cushion," pleaded Lilian. "The Virgin did not give birth to quadruplets." The vicar's wife caught sight of me and motioned for me to join her.

"Where's the vicar?" I asked, pulling over a folding chair. "Isn't he doing the narration?"

"Teddy's at the vicarage," Lilian said mournfully, "nursing a sore throat."

I gave her a sympathetic smile. "I'm sure he'll be better by Christmas Eve."

"The play won't," Lilian fretted. "It's a complete shambles, Lori. Mr. Farnham keeps falling off the stage, Peggy Kitchen jingles with every step, and Lady Eleanor insists on sicking up and fainting. If the play goes ahead as planned, we'll be prosecuted for heresy."

I murmured encouraging words about bad dress rehearsals making for wonderful performances, and she eventually regained her composure.

"Listen to me," she said, shamefaced, "having my little moan while the poor gentleman you found in your drive is fighting for his life. How is he, Lori?"

As I filled Lilian in on Kit Smith's progress, the sound of the sewing machine ceased, Jasper Taxman set aside his paintbrush, and a small knot of villagers gathered around to listen in.

"He's still unconscious," I concluded, "but he's stable, so I guess there's room for hope."

"There's always room for hope," Lilian said. "Teddy has been praying for him and will continue to do so."

Peggy Kitchen grunted. "He won't need too many prayers, not with the medical attention he's getting. Flew him to the Radcliffe, didn't you, Lori?"

"The lane was blocked with snow. It was the only way to get him to the hospital," I repeated patiently.

"I wouldn't have taken such trouble over a man like that," croaked Able Farnham. "I would've run him off."

"How?" I said. "He couldn't even walk."

"Might've been playing possum," Able Farnham said wisely.

"Didn't he frighten you?" asked George Wetherhead, leaning on his cane.

"No," I lied. "Why should he—"

"You're too trusting, Lori," chided Sally Pyne.

"He might've been an escaped convict," Christine Peacock pointed out.

"You never know, these days," her husband chimed in.

"He isn't—" I began, but Sally Pyne cut me off.

"It's the germs I'd worry about," she declared, peering at her own plump, spotless hands. "Everyone knows that tramps are a filthy lot."

"That's right," said Peggy Kitchen. "You might've exposed your sons to any number of diseases. Or nits. Didn't think of that, did you?"

"He's not—" I tried again, but this time Jasper Taxman jumped in.

"You were taking a great risk," he said judiciously. "Men of his sort are notoriously unstable."

"Thieves, the lot of them," quavered Able Farnham. "I had one pinch tomatoes from my bins once. In broad daylight."

"He must've been starving, to thieve *your* tomatoes," said a voice from the back of the room.

We all swung around to see who had issued the insult. Mr. Barlow stood in the doorway, his usually good-natured eyes smoldering. Buster crouched at his heels, growling softly.

"Listen to yourselves," said Mr. Barlow, his lip curling in disgust. "Tearing someone down when you don't know the first thing about him." He stepped into the room. "My dad was on the tramp back in the thirties, when times were hard, and he wasn't filthy, crazy, or a thief."

"It's not the thirties anymore," Jasper Taxman pointed out.

"Times are still hard, for some," retorted Mr. Barlow. He shook a finger at the group. "I wish the poor bugger'd come to my door. I'd've given him more than a kick in the backside and the sharp edge of my tongue, which is all he would've gotten from you lot." He looked defiantly from face to face, but his next words were addressed to me. "You give Kit Smith my best when he wakes up, Lori. You tell him if he needs a job, there's one waiting for him here in Finch."

"I will, Mr. Barlow," I said.

"As for the rest of you . . ." Mr. Barlow folded his arms, then turned on his heel. "C'mon, Buster. We're going home. There's a bad smell in here."

"Well, *really*," murmured Peggy Kitchen, when Mr. Barlow was safely out of earshot. "There was no need for *that*."

Lilian Bunting stood. "You're wrong, Mrs. Kitchen. There was a great need." I saw no sign of meekness in her manner as she squared off against the empress of Finch. "Since Teddy can't be here to run through the narration, I have decided to cancel tonight's rehearsal."

Peggy's false beard twitched ominously. "You can't—"

"I believe you'll find I can," Lilian declared.

There was a moment of shocked silence, followed by the sound of shuffling feet as the villagers edged away from Peggy Kitchen.

Lilian seemed to take no notice. "We will meet again on Monday night, as scheduled," she continued. "In the meantime, I would like each of you to study the narration carefully. Ask yourselves what kind of person would refuse shelter on a cold winter's night to a young, impoverished couple expecting their first child." The mild-mannered, scholarly woman folded her script and smacked it sharply against the palm of her hand. "And I shall expect to see all of you at church tomorrow."

Peggy Kitchen gathered up her red velvet gown and jingled indignantly to the women's dressing area. The others dispersed more quietly, but they favored Lilian with resentful glances as they went.

The last thing I heard before leaving the schoolhouse was Lilian saying, with steely determination, "And there will be *no sicking up!*"

"Why were the villagers so vicious?" I asked Aunt Dimity. The cottage was still and silent. Emma had left three hours ago, and Willis, Sr., was sleeping fitfully in the master bedroom. I'd bunked down on the rollaway bed in the nursery, but the memory of the villagers' attack on Kit had made sleep impossible. I was upset, and I'd come downstairs to the study, hoping that Dimity would help untie the knots in my stomach. "I mean, I wasn't wild about finding Kit in the drive, but I didn't wish him any harm. It's as if the villagers feel threatened by him."

They do. Aunt Dimity's handwriting spun across the page

in a soothingly familiar rhythm. *He reminds them of what they fear most.*

"Crime?" I said.

Poverty. You must remember, Lori, that most of your neighbors lived through the Great Depression. They know what it is to have only one pair of shoes, to be cold without hope of warmth, to go to bed hungry. They resent Kit for reminding them of a time they'd rather forget.

My gaze drifted from the page as the sound returned, the howl of a bitter wind driving sleet and snow before it like a scourge. I shuddered, pressed my fingers to my forehead, as if to push the sound away, and forced myself to look back at the journal.

Apart from that, Dimity had written, *your neighbors are getting on in years. It's all too easy for the elderly to imagine themselves slipping through the cracks and sliding into an impoverished old age. They fear what they once were, and they fear what they might become.*

"And fear makes them suspicious and cruel," I said slowly.

You mustn't judge them too harshly, Lori. They're good people, at heart. Once they overcome their fears, they'll do what's right, you'll see. Now, tell me what you've learned about Kit Smith since we last spoke.

I looked toward the hallway. "Sorry, Dimity," I said, with forced nonchalance, "but I've got to go. William's out of bed again. I may have to tie him down this time."

Go, look after your father-in-law. But come back soon.

I closed the blue journal and stared into the middle distance, recalling the resentment I'd felt at Kit's intrusion into my carefully planned holiday. I was the last person on earth qualified to judge my neighbors.

I had too much in common with them.

13

On Sunday morning I made sure that Willis, Sr., was resting comfortably, then strapped the twins into the Mercedes and took off for Saint George's. It had been nearly a week since Kit Smith had slipped silently into my life, and I felt the need for spiritual sustenance.

The church was unusually crowded. Peggy Kitchen and Jasper Taxman sat in the front row, Mr. Barlow sat in the back, and the Peacocks took up half a pew near the baptismal font. Sally Pyne helped Able Farnham to a place on the center aisle, and Lilian Bunting sat before the pulpit, where her husband could look to her for encouragement during his less than inspiring sermons.

The moment I spotted Lilian, I knew that something strange was afoot. She should have been greeting the parishioners, who were still streaming through the side door, but instead she was already seated, with her back to the congregation, speaking to no one. I wondered fleetingly if she was still upset over the villagers' mean-spirited remarks about Kit, then let the thought go, distracted by Will's interest in my hymnal.

Saint George's was resplendent. An imposing arrangement of silvery ferns rose from the Norman font, and Christmas roses set off by sprigs of holly decorated the altar. Evergreen garlands climbed the stone pillars, and the air was filled with the aromatic fragrance of yew and cypress.

The Victorian crèche, with the manger as yet empty, sat on a bed of sweet-smelling straw in the chancel, and as the organist played the first notes of the voluntary, I felt a glimmer of the contentment I'd hoped the season would bring. When the vicar mounted the pulpit to give his sermon, the twins and I settled back, with the rest of the congregation, to enjoy a pleasant doze. Theodore Bunting had come to Finch from a tough London parish and had never displayed the slightest inclination to re-create the fraught atmosphere he'd left behind. His sermons were, as a rule, low-key enough to serve as lullabies.

"On this, the fourth Sunday in Advent," he began, "I would like to speak to you of a certain visitor who recently passed through our community."

Heads that had begun to droop rose instantly. Everyone knew what the vicar was talking about—news of Kit's passage had spread to the farthest reaches of the parish—but no one had expected to hear a sermon on the subject. Then, too, there was an odd note in the vicar's voice, a sharpness that would, in anyone else, have signified anger.

"He was a stranger to our village," the vicar continued, "a poor man dressed in ragged clothes. He was hungry, yet he asked no one for food. He was ill, yet he asked for no one's help. Had he done so, I fear, he would have been hard-pressed to find so much as a crumb of kindness among us."

Mr. Barlow gave an audible *harrumph,* and unhappy glances were exchanged among those who'd attended the previous night's rehearsal.

The vicar leaned forward, his mild gray eyes flashing like unsheathed swords as he surveyed his flock. "He was a poor man and a stranger, and therefore not worthy of our kindness. The poor, as we all know, are a filthy lot—diseased, dishonest, and deserving of their fate. And strangers, you'll agree, must be treated with suspicion."

Peggy Kitchen's neck turned red and the Peacocks squirmed self-consciously. Old Mr. Farnham loosened his collar, as though the church had become uncomfortably warm, and Sally Pyne stared, shamefaced, at the hymn-book in her lap.

The vicar took a deep breath and straightened to his full and impressive height. His voice, usually so soothing, cracked like a whip above our heads. "God bestowed upon us the gift of his only begotten Son, yet there are those here present today who would not bestow so much as a kind word upon a sick and starving stranger.

"As we celebrate the birth of our Lord, let us remember that in the eyes of God no man is poor, and no man is a stranger.

"In this season of rejoicing, let us be thankful for blessings received and eager to share those blessings with others.

"Let us see in the poorest among us the face of the Christ Child.

"In the name of the Father . . ."

A wide-awake and sober congregation held its collective breath as its stern-faced pastor descended from the pulpit. When he motioned for us to rise, we leapt to our feet as though the pews had caught fire. The vicar's wrath, so seldom unleashed, had jolted everyone from complacent Christmas daydreams. It was as if a lightning bolt had struck the church, searing consciences and illuminating souls.

It's Kit, I thought dazedly. The man made his way through the world as quietly as falling snow, yet everyone was stirred by his passage. Nurse Willoughby, Julian Bright, Anne Somerville, Luke Boswell, and now the vicar—each had been inspired by Kit Smith. It was as if he left a trail of goodness in his wake for the rest of us to follow.

Sunday passed in a blur of child minding, cookie baking, and caring for my father-in-law. By Monday morning, Willis, Sr., felt well enough to come downstairs, but I was, at best, a distracted companion. I thought vaguely, guiltily, that I should make an effort to brighten his day, but the lure of Kit Smith was stronger. I could concentrate on little else.

I couldn't understand why Miss Kingsley hadn't called. She'd never before taken so long to fulfill an assignment, and the delay was eating away at me. Finally, after putting the boys down for their naps, I went into the study, closed the door, and called Julian. The moment I said hello, he asked eagerly if I'd heard from Miss Kingsley.

"No, I . . ." I swallowed hard and cradled the phone with both hands. "I just wanted to touch base with you. Have you found anything out about Kit's father?"

"Nothing so far," he replied. "Any luck with the names on the scroll?"

I relayed the information Emma had gathered, along with some I'd gleaned from Luke Boswell. When I mentioned the number of fatalities Bomber Command had sustained, Julian gave a low whistle.

"Sixty thousand dead out of one hundred twenty-five thousand," he said. "I'd no idea that casualty rate was so high. You're becoming quite an expert on the subject." He paused. "I hope it's not casting too great a pall over your holidays."

"I'm all right." I wiped away a tear that had trickled, un-accountably, down my face.

A long moment of silence passed before Julian said quietly, "What's wrong, Lori?"

"Nothing." I sniffed. "My husband's in Boston, my father-in-law's sick, the Christmas tree's still in the garden shed, I haven't wrapped a single present, and Christmas is less than a week away." I rested my elbow on the desk and leaned my forehead on my hand. "And none of it matters. All I can think about is Kit."

"I'll be with you in less than an hour," said Julian.

"Julian, you don't have to——" I began, but he'd already hung up. I returned the phone to the cradle and nearly jumped out of my skin when it rang. I snatched it up, saying, "Julian?"

"No, Lori, it's me," said Miss Kingsley. "I have the information you requested. And I must say, it's fascinating."

"Christopher Smith was an inmate at the Heathermoor Asylum for approximately six months," Miss Kingsley began.

I closed my eyes and whispered, "No . . ."

"It doesn't mean he belonged there," Miss Kingsley said. "What I mean to say is, I don't think Kit Smith was in the asylum because he was ill."

"I don't understand," I said.

"I'll try to explain." I heard a rustle of paper, as if Miss Kingsley were assembling her notes. "The Heathermoor Asylum was located in Skellingthorpe, just outside Lincoln."

"*Was?*" I said quickly.

"If you'll allow me to continue . . ." Miss Kingsley said, a faint note of reproof in her voice.

"Sorry," I said. "Go on."

Miss Kingsley cleared her throat. "As I was saying, the Heathermoor Asylum was located in Lincolnshire. A privately run institution, it had been in existence for twenty-seven years when one Christopher Smith, aged thirty-eight, arrived on its doorstep and asked to be admitted."

"He volunteered to be shut up in a mental institution?" I said, incredulous.

"He did," said Miss Kingsley. "According to his file, he gave as his home address the Wayfarers' Refuge in Lincoln. He claimed to be suffering from recurrent bouts of depression and requested immediate admission."

I tried to imagine Kit presenting himself on the doorstep of a privately run asylum. What would they have made of his ragged clothes and wild hair?

"I can't believe they let him in," I said. "Didn't they require some sort of fee?"

"As a matter of fact, they required quite steep fees," Miss Kingsley said grimly, "but the admitting physician, Dr. Rosalind Chalmers, took pity on Kit. Her notes are most revealing. She was, apparently, beguiled by him."

"Welcome to the club," I muttered.

"Pardon?" said Miss Kingsley.

"Never mind," I said hastily. "Please, continue."

"Kit was, according to Dr. Chalmers, a model patient," said Miss Kingsley. "According to his records, he took his medication and stayed quietly in the background. He responded so well to his treatment that he was allowed to work as a file clerk in the main office."

"Is that all the treatment he received?" I asked. "Just pills?"

"Heathermoor offered nothing but pills." Miss Kingsley sniffed contemptuously. "Nothing but pills and bills. It was a disgrace. The final report of the investigatory commission—"

"Whoa," I interrupted. "Back up. What final report? What investigatory commission?"

"One month after Kit admitted himself to Heathermoor, certain government departments began to receive telephone calls from inside the asylum," said Miss Kingsley. "The caller reported unsanitary conditions, grossly inadequate diets, myriad cases of physical abuse, and an almost total absence of qualified staff."

"Any idea who made those reports?" I asked, gripping the telephone tightly.

"An anonymous source," said Miss Kingsley. "A *male* anonymous source. No one has been able to identify him."

He wouldn't have left a name, I thought. It's not his style.

"Thanks to those reports, the Heathermoor Asylum was shut down just over a year ago," said Miss Kingsley. "Some members of the staff were brought up on criminal charges; others were merely dismissed. The residents were relocated and the records dispersed. That's why it took so long—"

"Miss Kingsley," I broke in urgently, "what happened to Kit?"

"No one knows," she replied. "Apparently, one of the patient-transport vans broke down on its way to an institution in Cambridgeshire. In the ensuing confusion, Kit Smith simply disappeared."

Only to turn up at the church at Great Gransden, I thought, where he focused his attention on the problem of saving Blackthorne Farm.

"The authorities had their hands full, coping with the Heathermoor scandal," Miss Kingsley continued. "Since Kit wasn't considered dangerous to the population at large, he was never seriously pursued. As far as I can tell, he hasn't been admitted to any other institution since he released himself from Heathermoor."

I felt my throat constrict. I was absolutely certain that Kit had blown the whistle on the Heathermoor Asylum.

Miss Kingsley agreed. "The timing of Kit Smith's arrival and departure, and the fact that he had access to a telephone while working in the office, leads me to suspect strongly that he was the anonymous caller." She paused. "I should very much like to meet Mr. Smith. Have you any idea what became of him?"

"Yes," I said, "but it's kind of complicated."

"Perhaps you could fill me in on Friday," Miss Kingsley suggested. "Now I have yet another reason to look forward to your party."

I moaned softly. The Christmas Eve bash had slipped my mind along with everything else. "Do you have the phone number of the Wayfarers' Refuge in Lincoln?" I asked, and scribbled down the information as Miss Kingsley passed it along.

"Will Bill be at the party?" asked Miss Kingsley.

I stiffened. "He says he will. Why? What have you heard?"

"Rumor has it that the Collier estate is a frightful tangle," replied Miss Kingsley, "and I know how tenacious your husband can be when he's dealing with complicated wills. That being said," she concluded hastily, "I'm certain he'll be home in time for the party. He wouldn't dream of missing his sons' first Christmas."

I thanked Miss Kingsley for her help and hung up the phone, perturbed. I hadn't seriously considered the possibility of Bill spending Christmas in Boston, but if the Collier estate was a mess, he might very well feel compelled to stay on until he'd sorted it out. The Willis work ethic was as Puritan as Plymouth Rock.

I should have exploded. The mere idea of Bill missing Christmas at the cottage should have infuriated me, but instead a smile came, unbidden, to my lips. Who was I to criticize my husband? He, at least, was helping a cherished friend's widow, whereas I'd put Christmas on hold for the sake of a total stranger.

Yet Kit was no longer a stranger. In the past week he'd become as dear to me as Willis, Sr., and the more I learned about him, the dearer he became. I would have defended and protected him no matter what Miss Kingsley had discovered.

I thought of Kit's face, haloed by golden light, as if he'd brought his own radiance to the dimly lit cubicle, and knew that I was no longer content to find out why his path had intersected with mine. I wanted to know what had set him on his journey in the first place.

I stared down at the phone number Miss Kingsley had given me. I would call the Wayfarers' Refuge in Lincoln. I'd find someone who could tell me what Kit Smith had done before he'd set out for Skellingthorpe and the Heathermoor Asylum. If I went back far enough, I'd find Kit's starting point. There, perhaps, I would discover what had inspired his strange pilgrimage.

The phone was in my hand when I heard a knock at the study door and the sound of Willis, Sr.'s voice telling me that a visitor awaited me in the living room.

14

I flew down the hallway, hoping for a moment alone with Julian before Willis, Sr., joined us. I was embarrassed by the teary phone call that had summoned the priest to the cottage, and I didn't want him to mention it in front of my father-in-law.

As I came into the living room, Julian stepped toward me, his eyes clouded with anxiety.

"Lori," he said, "are you all right?"

"Please," I whispered urgently, "don't—" I stopped short as Willis, Sr., entered the room.

Julian's furrowed brow smoothed instantly. "I didn't want to run up the bill on your cell phone, Lori," he improvised, "so I dropped by to find out if you'd heard from Miss Kingsley yet."

I thanked him silently, then gave him a radiant smile. "She just called."

"Judging by the expression on your face, she must have been the bearer of glad tidings," Willis, Sr., observed.

"The gladdest," I said. "But it's a long story, and Julian looks as though he could do with a cup of tea—"

"Not burdock root, I trust," interrupted Willis, Sr., his patrician nose wrinkling in distaste.

"Earl Grey?" I offered.

"Splendid." Willis, Sr., cocked an ear toward the baby monitor. The twins were moving about in their cribs, which meant that naptime was over. "Father Bright," said Willis, Sr., turning to the priest, "would you care to help me with my grandsons?"

Julian's eyes met mine, then turned toward Willis, Sr. "I'd be delighted."

While the men went up to the nursery, I set up the twins' playpen in the kitchen and pulled out a pair of breadsticks for them to gum, then put the kettle on and piled angel cookies on a plate.

The boys preferred playing to eating after naptime, and Willis, Sr., would be content to sip tea and nibble a cookie, but I suspected that Julian would welcome a change of pace from Saint Benedict's "simple, nourishing meals." With that thought in mind, I made up a selection of finger sandwiches, warmed the chicken soup, and put out a loaf of crusty homemade bread and a pot of sweet butter.

Since the dining room was chockablock with unused Christmas decorations, I set the kitchen table, and when everything was ready, called the men into the kitchen. Rob accepted confinement in the playpen with his usual placidity, but Will, fascinated by Julian's goatee, required an extra five minutes in the priest's arms before he would consent to his imprisonment.

A look of rapture came to Julian's face when he caught the soup's rich aroma, so I filled a bowl for him and pushed the finger sandwiches his way. I had the satisfaction of watching him go through three bowls of soup, two-thirds of the sandwiches, and half the loaf of bread while I told the tale of Kit Smith's stay at the now defunct Heathermoor Asylum.

"After he closed down Heathermoor," I concluded, "he turned up in Great Gransden, where he saved Blackthorne Farm. Then it was on to Oxford—"

"—where he saved my life." Julian shook his head, bemused. "I've heard it said that angels walk among us. Perhaps one lies in the Radcliffe Infirmary."

"Skellingthorpe," Willis, Sr., said thoughtfully. "Did you say that the Heathermoor Asylum was located at Skellingthorpe? In Lincolnshire?"

"That's right," I replied. "Skellingthorpe's a sort of suburb of Lincoln now. Apparently, Kit stayed at the Wayfarers' Refuge in Lincoln before he checked himself into the asylum. Why? Does Skellingthorpe mean something to you?"

"Possibly. But I must first check my facts." Willis, Sr., excused himself and left the kitchen.

Julian reached for an angel cookie. "I've been meaning to tell you," he said, "that these confections of yours are heavenly. You could make a fortune if you ever decided to sell them."

I blushed with pleasure, but gave credit where credit was due. "My father invented the recipe."

Julian finished the cookie in two bites, then brushed the crumbs from his fingers. "Will you be seeing your parents over Christmas?"

"No." I got up to clear the table, dreading the awkward pause that always followed my next words. "They're both dead. My mom died a few years ago and my father died when I was very young."

"And you're carrying on the family tradition." Julian brought his soup bowl to me at the sink. "I must say that it's a delicious one."

I glanced up at him gratefully. The subject of death was, more often than not, a guaranteed conversation-stopper, but Julian had defused the awkward moment with grace and a touch of humor. On top of that, he hadn't scolded me for dragging him out to the cottage for no apparent reason. Perhaps, I thought, Kit wasn't the only angel walking among us.

I started to take the soup bowl from him, but Julian kept hold of it.

"Lori," he said, "what's troubling you?"

"Nothing," I assured him. "I'm fine."

Julian eyed me doubtfully. "You didn't sound fine when you rang me."

I ducked my head. "Sorry about that. I guess I was just anxious to hear from Miss Kingsley."

"Is that all?" Julian asked.

"What else would it be?" I pulled the soup bowl from him and put it in the sink, then stood staring down at the soapy water. How could I tell Julian what was troubling me when I wasn't sure myself?

"Lori," Julian began, but he fell silent at the sound of Willis, Sr.'s voice.

"I thought so," called Willis, Sr. "I knew Skellingthorpe sounded familiar." He entered the kitchen brandishing the book I'd borrowed from Luke Boswell.

"Is that what you've been reading?" I asked, wiping my hands on a towel.

"I found it on your bedside table," Willis, Sr., informed me. "It is a general history of Bomber Command," he explained to Julian. "I believe it contains information pertinent to our discussion of Mr. Smith."

Julian and I stood over Willis, Sr., as he opened the book to a map labeled *Bomber Command: Group Headquarters and Main Airfields, February 1944*. The black dots denoting bomber bases stretched all the way from Durham in the north to Hertfordshire in the south. There was even a base at Lossiemouth, on the northeast coast of Scotland.

"You see?" said Willis, Sr., pointing to the map. "There was a bomber base at Skellingthorpe, one of a cluster of bases located in Lincolnshire." He tapped the page with the tip of his index finger. "If Mr. Smith were planning to tour airfields in Lincolnshire, he would do well to select Lincoln as a jumping-off point."

Julian nodded. "Just as he chose Blackthorne Farm as a jumping-off point for the Cambridgeshire airfields. Is that what you're saying?"

Willis, Sr., leaned back in his chair and tented his fingers over his pin-striped waistcoat. "I am merely suggesting that the scope of your search may be too narrow. Thanks to Mrs. Somerville and Miss Kingsley, we can now trace Mr. Smith's movements to two parts of the country that contain large numbers of abandoned airfields— Lincolnshire and Cambridgeshire. If he was, as you posit, praying for the men listed on the scroll, I would suggest that he had as his goal the entire network of bomber bases."

"But the scroll contains thousands of names." I gestured toward the map. "And there must be over a hundred bomber bases."

"Those are simply the main airfields," Willis, Sr., reminded me. "The map does not account for subsidiary fields."

"But if Kit traveled to each one of them . . ." I sat abruptly, feeling slightly dazed. "He must have been on the road for *years*."

"It would explain his physical deterioration," said Willis, Sr.

"I agree," said Julian. "An itinerant life tends to age one prematurely."

"But *why?*" I demanded. "Why did he live an itinerant life? Anne Somerville said that he was well educated. Why didn't he get a job and buy a car and drive from base to base? Why did he make it so hard on himself?"

"One may as well ask why he risked his life to come to the cottage," said Willis, Sr. "The answers, I fear, are not self-evident. Perhaps, when Mr. Smith emerges from his coma, he will provide them."

"I can't wait that long." I drummed my fingers on the table. "I'm going to call the refuge in Lincoln right now. Or maybe we should just drive up there, Julian. It's not that far, is it? And it'd be worth the trip if someone at the refuge knows—" I flinched as Willis, Sr., snapped the book shut with a bang.

"Lori." Willis, Sr., stood and faced me. "Your curiosity about Mr. Smith is understandable, but you cannot go to Lincoln."

I stared at him, puzzled. "Why not?"

Willis, Sr., spoke patiently, as if to a small child. "Today is December twentieth. Four days from now, thirty guests will be descending on the cottage, expecting to find festive food as well as festive decor. Unless you are content to serve them rewarmed chicken soup and welcome them to a Christmas party without a Christmas tree, I do not think you will have time to travel to Lincoln."

"Oh," I said.

"Your father-in-law's quite right, Lori," Julian chimed in. "I'll ring the Wayfarers' Refuge. If need be, I'll drive to Lincoln. But you must stay here, where you're needed.

Mr. Willis," he added, taking up the book on Bomber Command, "would you mind if I borrowed this?"

"Not at all," said Willis, Sr. "I believe you will find the chapter on the Pathfinder force particularly interesting. Are you familiar with the Pathfinders? . . ."

While the two men talked, I tried to reconcile myself to the thought of staying at home. I couldn't argue with Willis, Sr.'s logic—it would take me at least three days to prepare for the Christmas Eve party—but something in me balked at letting Julian carry on without me. Still, what choice did I have? I was, as Julian had pointed out, needed at home.

"You'll let me know the minute you find out anything," I said to the priest.

"The very second." Julian cocked an ear toward the hallway as the clock in the study chimed the hour. "Good heavens, is that the time? I'm afraid I must be off."

"And I must prepare for tonight's rehearsal," said Willis, Sr. "It is our last before our performance on Christmas Eve."

"Are you sure you're feeling well enough?" I asked him.

"After hearing your account of the vicar's sermon," said Willis, Sr., "I would not miss tonight's rehearsal for the world. If you will excuse me, Father Bright . . ."

Julian watched Willis, Sr., go, then turned to say good-bye to the boys. As I came to stand beside him, Will lifted his arms to the priest and chirped, "Papa."

Julian laughed heartily. "That is, without doubt, the finest compliment I've ever been paid."

"I'll get your jacket," I said, and hurried down the hall, blushing crimson.

Julian was still grinning as he slipped into his leather jacket, but as he turned to say good-bye, his face grew serious. He looked down at me in silence for a moment, then reached out to cup my chin in his hand. "You're sure you're all right?"

"Uh-huh," I managed, as the warmth from his hand spread downward.

"I still have your cell phone," he said. "If you need me, night or day . . ." He dropped his hand and opened the front door. "Ring me."

I nodded, not trusting myself to speak. I stood in the doorway until Saint Christopher was out of sight, then returned to the kitchen and looked pointedly at Will. "That's *Father* Bright," I told him, brushing my knuckles lightly across my chin. "Not *Papa*."

15

I was in bed and asleep before Willis, Sr., returned from the rehearsal, so I didn't hear about it until he joined me in the nursery early the next morning. Rob was fully dressed and playing in his crib while I sat on the floor, dressing his brother.

"What a beautiful morning!" Willis, Sr., exclaimed. He lifted Rob from the crib and waltzed him to the window. "Have you ever seen such a beautiful day?"

"Why do I have a beautiful feeling that everything's going your way?" I pulled Will's pants up over his fresh diaper and reached for his socks. "The rehearsal went well, did it?"

Willis, Sr., kissed Rob's nose and beamed out at the world in general. "It could not have been more satisfactory. Mrs. Kitchen's costume no longer jingles, Mr. Farnham did not once topple from the stage, and Lady Eleanor's performance was flawless."

No more sicking up, I thought, chuckling softly.

"Yet it must be said," Willis, Sr., continued, "that the

most pleasing aspect of the entire evening was Mrs. Bunting's transformation. Everyone spoke of it, but I believe Mr. Barlow put it best. 'The vicar's sermon,' he said, 'put a bit of snap in Lilian's stockings.' "

"William!" I protested, laughing.

A distant look came to Willis, Sr.'s gray eyes as he turned to face me. "I wish you could have seen her, Lori, ordering Mrs. Kitchen to remove the drapery rings from the hem of her costume. Mrs. Bunting was"—he struggled to find a word adequate to the situation—"*magnificent.*"

"No comments on your American accent?" I hazarded.

"None at all," Willis, Sr., replied. "Mrs. Bunting is a most discerning woman and a brilliant director." He sat on the window seat and shifted Rob to his lap. "A humanitarian as well."

"She should be," I said, twiddling Will's toes. "She's the vicar's wife."

"It was in her capacity as director, however, that Mrs. Bunting made the unilateral decision to donate the play's proceeds to Saint Benedict's Hostel for Transient Men."

I straightened. "How did she know about Saint Benedict's? I didn't tell her about it."

Willis, Sr., took a sudden interest in Rob's fingernails. "I may have mentioned Father Bright's predicament to her, in passing. I fear that our modest donation will do little to remedy the situation at Saint Benedict's, but one must do what one can, mustn't one?"

"Yes," I said, eyeing him thoughtfully. "One must."

Willis, Sr., bounced Rob on his knee. "I wish to move back into the nursery," he announced. "I am fully recovered from my recent indisposition, and the master bedroom is much too far away from my grandsons."

"We'll move you back tonight," I promised. "But before

then we're going to bring a little Christmas to the cottage. I'll whip up a batch of gingerbread men after breakfast, then we'll get cracking on those decorations."

"I look forward to assisting you," Willis, Sr., said, rising. "My staff has never permitted me to decorate my own home. . . ."

By noon it was clear that the Christmas fairy had put a curse on the cottage. Every one of my gingerbread men burned to a crisp, filling the air with smoke instead of the spicy-sweet aroma I'd intended. The living tree insisted on listing to one side, no matter how carefully we adjusted its root ball, and Willis, Sr., whacked his thumb with the hammer he was using to hang the mistletoe. I don't know what the boys made of certain exclamations they may have overheard, but I prayed they wouldn't repeat them to Bill.

We achieved very little after lunch, thanks to a steady stream of villagers bearing gifts. The vicar's sermon and the snap in Lilian's stockings had evidently had an impact on the community's group conscience, because the gifts weren't meant for us. They were meant for Kit.

Sally Pyne brought a box of hand-dipped chocolates from her tearoom; the Peacocks, a bottle of homemade brandy from the pub. Able Farnham dropped off a basket of fruit from his greengrocer's shop, and George Wetherhead delivered a pile of old magazines.

"I've spent a fair amount of time in hospitals," said Mr. Wetherhead, leaning heavily on his three-pronged cane. "The days'll pass more quickly if the young chap has something to read."

The most amazing gift of all came from Peggy Kitchen. The doughty widow had assembled a full set of winter clothing from the stock in the Emporium——wool socks, insulated boots, a warm sweater, heavy trousers, leather gloves, even a down-filled, hooded parka.

"If the sizes aren't right," Peggy said gruffly, "tell Mr. Smith he can exchange them the next time he's in Finch."

"I will, Peggy," I told her, and my gruffness came from a tightening throat.

Aunt Dimity's wise prediction chimed inside my head all afternoon. *They're good people, at heart,* she'd written. *Once they overcome their fears, they'll do what's right, you'll see.* I did see, and what I saw made me realize that I still had a lot to learn about——and from——my neighbors.

I sent each of them away with a box of angel cookies, and felt a measure of satisfaction at having carried out at least one of my father's traditions. As I set their gifts aside, though, I felt a rising sense of restlessness.

Their concern for Kit had rekindled my own. It had been lingering just below the surface all day long. Now it came back full force, filling me with frustration and making it impossible for me focus on any of the tasks Willis, Sr., and I had set for ourselves. Between his lack of experience and my lack of enthusiasm, the decorations went up in a somewhat haphazard fashion. If the Christmas fairy's curse had spoiled the morning, my own impatience tainted the afternoon.

When the telephone rang in the middle of dinner, I ran to answer it. "Julian?" I said eagerly.

"Sorry to disappoint you, love," said Bill, "but it's only me."

I gave a shaky laugh and wondered what was wrong with me. It was the second time in as many days that I'd snatched up the phone, hoping to hear Julian's voice.

"I'm never disappointed to hear from you," I told my

husband. "But I'll be a lot happier when you're not three thousand miles away. When are you coming home?"

"I wanted to surprise you by coming home today," Bill said, "but an ice storm's paralyzed Boston. Logan's been shut down for the past twenty-four hours."

I groaned and leaned my head on my hand. "When I write this chapter in my autobiography, I'm going to call it 'The Blizzards That Ate Christmas.' "

"I've chartered a flight," Bill said quickly. "The pilot's assured me that we'll take off as soon as the runways are open. I promise you, Lori, I'll be home by Christmas if I have to swim the Atlantic."

I took a deep breath and let it out slowly. "All I care about is that you get home safely and in one piece, Bill. Don't worry about Christmas. We won't start it without you."

I hung up the phone and looked over at the mantelpiece, where the lacy glass star rested in splendid isolation. Willis, Sr., had offered to put it on the top of the badly listing tree, but I'd forbidden it. Crowning the tree would be Bill's privilege, just as it had been my father's.

I checked in with Emma the following morning, to see if she'd discovered anything about the owner of Kit Smith's medals, but she'd been too busy baking to sit down at the computer. It took an effort of the will to keep from insisting that she put Christmas aside for Kit's sake. Not everyone, I reminded myself, shared my concern for his well-being.

I spent the rest of the day cremating gingerbread men and examining Kit's scroll with a magnifying glass, searching for a Christopher Smith. An eyestrain headache and the smell of smoke in the kitchen forced me to abandon the search after the first twenty-five pages.

Julian's call didn't come until late evening.

"I hope I didn't wake you," he said.

"Never mind about that," I said, switching on the bedside lamp. "Did you speak with anyone in Lincoln?"

Julian laughed. "In Lincoln, York, Durham, Lossiemouth, and London, among other places. Your phone bill's going to be astronomical, I'm afraid, but I think you'll consider it a worthy investment. . . ."

Julian had hit upon the brilliant notion of using the map Willis, Sr., had shown us as a guide to Kit's travels. My suggestion about contacting the refuge network had come in handy, too.

"I went with the assumption that Kit would stay in towns or villages near former bomber bases," Julian explained, "and that he'd use shelters like Saint Benedict's when they were available." By calling shelters located in the vicinity of bases, Julian had pieced together a profile of Kit's movements over the past four years.

"I don't know how many people I've spoken with today," said Julian, "but those who met Kit, no matter how long ago, remember him."

"He does make an impression," I commented, glancing at the canvas carryall.

"When a shelter wasn't available near a cluster of bases," Julian continued, "Kit must have arranged some other form of inexpensive lodging."

"Like finding a job that included room and board," I put in, "as he did at Blackthorne Farm."

"Precisely," said Julian. "That's why there are certain gaps in the story."

I smiled. "You mean to say that you didn't call every farm between Hertfordshire and Durham?"

"I didn't have to," Julian replied. "Not after I spoke with the chap who runs the soup kitchen in Lossiemouth. He told me that Kit had compared his soup kitchen to one run by a C of E church in London—Saint Joseph's, in Stepney." The priest's voice began to vibrate with barely suppressed excitement. "When I called Saint Joseph's, the woman who answered the phone told me that the vicar, a man named Phillip Raywood, *knows Kit's family*."

I bent over the phone, wishing Julian were in the room with me instead of somewhere in the ether. "Did you speak with Phillip Raywood?"

"Alas," said Julian, "he was gone for the day. But I've made arrangements to meet with him at Saint Joseph's to-morrow evening." He hesitated. "I don't suppose there's any chance of your coming with me."

I thumped my pillow with a clenched fist. I hated being a bystander, watching Julian from the sidelines, but there was nothing else I could do.

"I can't, Julian," I said forlornly. "I keep burning the gingerbread men, and there's still the wreath to hang on the front door, and presents to wrap . . ." My words trailed off in a disappointed mumble.

"Forgive me," said Julian. "I shouldn't have proposed the idea. What you're doing is far more important than what I plan to do tomorrow. Family traditions must be nurtured, Lori, if they're to . . ." His voice faded suddenly.

"Julian?" I said. "Are you still there?" I strained to catch his words, but his reply was garbled.

"Sorry . . . speak with you soon . . ." His voice grew fainter and fainter, then faded completely.

"Good luck," I said softly, and hung up, wanting to kick myself. Why hadn't I given Julian the recharger when I'd given him the phone? The myriad calls he'd made must have drained the battery dry.

Sighing, I crawled to the end of the bed and pulled the canvas carryall into my arms. I'd dreamt of Kit last night, as I had every night that week. He'd been on the bridle path, riding a high-stepping black stallion, his long hair streaming behind him, the reins taut in his beautiful hands.

When he reached the cottage, the horse reared and Kit tumbled to the ground. As he fell, the stallion twisted grotesquely and dissolved, shrinking from view, leaving Kit on his knees, gazing at me through the brightly lit bow window. While I beamed out at the falling snow, Kit crumpled beneath my lilac bushes, clutching Anne Somerville's little brown horse in hands blackened by frostbite.

I'd awakened in tears, and now it seemed as if I'd fall asleep the same way. The knowledge that Julian might soon meet Kit's family without me was very hard to bear. Anne Somerville had said that Kit's father was dead, but his mother might still be alive, and if she was, she'd be frantic to know what had happened to her son. She'd welcome Julian with open arms.

Unless she felt uncomfortable talking to a man.

Or mistrusted Roman Catholic priests.

I laid my cheek briefly against the carryall, then returned it to the blanket chest and headed for the study. I needed to consult Aunt Dimity.

". . . So Julian could go all the way to London and meet with Phillip Raywood and find Kit's mom and still come back empty-handed," I concluded.

Dimity responded without hesitation. *Then you must go to London.*

I gazed at the words doubtfully. "What about nurturing family traditions?"

Family traditions are an exercise in futility if one's heart's not in them. Your heart is transparently occupied elsewhere.

"My heart's not the issue," I insisted. "Kit is. The only thing holding me back is William. I don't think he'll approve of my trip."

If this mission is as important to you as you say it is, I believe William will understand. There is something I'd like to know, however, for my own peace of mind.

"What's that?' I said.

Why is it so important to you?

I pressed the heel of my hand to my forehead, to ward off the howling wind, and slowly closed the journal.

As it turned out, Dimity and I were both right. Willis, Sr., wasn't happy about my plan to meet up with Julian in London, but he didn't question my need to do so. He was so understanding, in fact, that I didn't bridle at the one condition he placed upon my going.

"You will take the train to London," he stated flatly. "My son would never forgive me if I allowed you to drive there."

16

I knew that Julian would give me a lift home in Saint Christopher, so I hitched a ride to Oxford the next day with Derek Harris, who was headed there to consult on a construction project. He dropped me at the train station and I plunged into the fray.

With less than two shopping days left until Christmas, panic had set in. The train to London was packed, and Paddington Station was a frantic anthill of last-minute shoppers. I clutched Kit's canvas carryall to me, kept a firm grip on my shoulder bag, and elbowed my way through the throng to the long line at the cab stand. Forty minutes later, I was on my way to Saint Joseph's Church.

The driver, an East Indian, knew Saint Joseph's well. "It's round the corner from my sister's flat," he said. He eyed me in the rearview mirror, as if wondering why an American tourist would spend the day before Christmas Eve in the lower reaches of Stepney instead of Harrods' hallowed halls. "You sure you want to go there?"

I told him that I was.

The journey seemed to take forever. The East End's narrow lanes, choked with traffic at the best of times, had turned into a slowly shifting parking lot. People of every color and ethnicity crowded the sidewalks and spilled into the streets as we crawled past brightly lit shops whose signs were written in languages I couldn't even identify, much less understand.

"Snow again tonight," the driver told me, making conversation while we waited at a stoplight. "Never seen so much snow in all my days here. Makes me wish I could go home again." He slouched resignedly and inched the cab forward as the light changed.

Eventually, we turned onto a dimly lit street lined with massive apartment buildings. I gazed up at a solitary window framed with blinking Christmas lights and ducked when a hail of snowballs battered the cab's roof. The driver rolled his window down and bellowed at a pair of scruffy teenagers, who made predictable hand gestures and fled into the darkness between two buildings, laughing maniacally.

"This is no place for you, missus," said the driver, closing his window.

"I'll be fine once we get to Saint Joseph's," I told him. "I'm meeting with the vicar."

"Ah, Father Raywood." The driver nodded. "He's a good man. Too good for this place. I keep telling my sister to leave, but does she listen? Not likely. Here you are, missus."

And suddenly, there was Saint Joseph's, a redbrick Victorian pile surrounded on three sides by ten-foot brick walls and well lit by security floodlights. The church was pug-ugly—blackened by soot and striped with garish bands of rough-cut stone, its stained glass done in unappealing hues of orange and blue—yet it somehow retained

an air of dignity that the shoddy postwar buildings surrounding it would never achieve.

I paid the cabbie and walked quickly toward a side entrance, where two men loitered, smoking cigarettes and
stamping their feet against the cold. They were dressed as
Kit had been, in grubby greatcoats and frayed trousers,
and when I asked where I might find Father Raywood, they
replied in voices as gravelly as Rupert's.

"Try the soup kitchen," growled one, jutting his stubbly
chin toward the door.

"Downstairs," growled the other.

"Thanks," I said, and hastened inside, bracing myself for
another grim journey through damp and darkened corridors enlivened by scurrying roaches and the pitter-patter
of tiny, clawed feet.

To my amazement—and vast relief—Saint Joseph's was
nothing like Saint Benedict's. The square foyer, the wide
staircase, and the tiled passage leading to the basement
dining area were white-painted and brightly lit, and the air
was filled with the aroma of roast turkey instead of the
stink of boiled cabbage.

The dining room was equally well maintained, but here
the walls were hung with paper chains, silver bells, and
twinkling lights, and a gaily decorated artificial tree tow-
ered in the far corner. As I entered the dining room, a uni-
formed cleanup crew was at work, mopping up after what
must have been the last meal of the day. And there, in the
midst of the bustle, with a wet rag in his hand and the
sleeves of his black turtleneck pushed up, was Julian.

"Lori?" He stood very still when he saw me, as if he
thought he might be hallucinating. "What are you doing
here?"

I hitched the canvas carryall higher on my shoulder and
walked over to him. "I couldn't stay away."

His brow furrowed. "But what about—"

"Family traditions?" I said. "I'll take care of them when I get home tonight." I shrugged impatiently. "What about Phillip Raywood? Have you spoken with him?"

"Not yet. He's reading evensong in the Lady Chapel." Julian leaned closer, a delicious twinkle in his eyes. "He's *very* High Church. I feel quite at home."

"Well, I can't stand around while everyone else is working." I unbuttoned my coat. "Show me where to stash my stuff, then tell me what needs doing."

A half hour later, Julian and I were alone in the kitchen, sipping well-earned cups of tea. The cleanup crew had gone, leaving the place spotless. Julian surveyed the stainless-steel countertops and the restaurant-quality appliances, sighing dismally.

"I have a confession to make," he said. "I covet Father Raywood's kitchen."

"I forgive you, my son." The kitchen's well-oiled swing doors swung shut as a man breezed into the room, his hand extended. "Phillip Raywood," he said, by way of introduction.

The introduction was unnecessary, because, unlike Julian, Phillip Raywood looked like a priest. He was tall, austere, and angular, with a naturally tonsured head and a pair of wire-rimmed glasses that seemed custom-made to go with his clerical collar and ankle-length cassock. He betrayed a hint of disappointment as he surveyed his Catholic counterpart's more casual garb.

"I'm sorry to have kept you waiting," he said, after Julian and I had introduced ourselves. "I was told that you have news of Christopher Smith. He's well, I trust?"

"I'm afraid not," said Julian. "In fact, he's in hospital, seriously ill."

"May God have mercy on him." As he uttered the

blessing, Father Raywood gazed around the kitchen, as though taking stock of the equipment. "My assistant, Father Danos, will be along shortly," he said. "I would be grateful if you would wait until he— Ah, Andrew, there you are."

A second Anglican priest had come into the kitchen. Andrew Danos was younger, shorter, and beefier than Phillip Raywood, but he, too, was dressed in exemplary High Church fashion. He shook hands with Julian and me, then pulled two chairs up to the table and poured tea for Father Raywood. There was no doubt about the pecking order at Saint Joseph's.

"Normally, I would invite you to the vicarage," said Father Raywood, as he took his seat, "but this is a far more suitable place in which to discuss Christopher Smith. If it weren't for him, you see, Saint Joseph's wouldn't have such fine facilities."

"He . . . installed them?" Julian ventured.

"Certainly not." Father Raywood seemed to find the suggestion ridiculous. "He *paid* for them."

Father Danos, as if sensing confusion in the air, spoke up. "Perhaps, Father, if we told our guests how we came to meet Mr. Smith . . ."

"Yes, very well, begin at the beginning." Father Raywood sipped from his teacup, touched a cloth napkin to his lips, and began.

"Christopher Smith first came to Saint Joseph's four years ago, in February. There was the promise of snow in the air that night, just as there is tonight. Do you remember, Andrew?"

"As if it were yesterday," said Father Danos. "We were struggling to keep the soup kitchen open," he explained. "We're not a wealthy parish, but the need for our services grows more desperate every year, particularly in the winter months."

"Christopher Smith sat at a corner table at the far end of the dining room," Father Raywood went on. "He ate nothing, simply watched the other men. He worried me, frankly. He seemed dazed and was clearly out of place."

"What made him seem out of place?" I asked.

Father Raywood seemed puzzled by my question. "The men who patronize our soup kitchen do not, as a rule, patronize Savile Row."

"He was well dressed?" I said, recalling Anne Somerville's claim that Kit had been born to money.

"He was extremely well dressed," Father Raywood confirmed, "and strikingly handsome. His hands were manicured, his hair freshly barbered—he was clearly a man of means." A frown puckered his brow. "As I said, he worried me, so I sent Andrew over to have a word with him."

"I asked if I could help him in any way," said Father Danos, "and he looked up at me." The young priest's face grew troubled. "Such a look. As if he'd lost the one thing he loved most in the world. 'No,' he told me, 'I don't think you can help me. In any way.' "

"You remember his exact words?" said Julian.

"I'll never forget them. His voice was . . . quite beautiful. And so very sad." Father Danos stared briefly into the middle distance, then went on. "He began to leave, but turned back to ask if our church was dedicated to Saint Joseph of Cupertino. I told him no, that our Saint Joseph was the husband of the Holy Virgin. 'So I got that wrong, too,' he murmured, and left."

Father Raywood eyed his assistant somberly. "Andrew was deeply disturbed by the encounter, and—"

"I felt I'd failed him," Father Danos interrupted. "His eyes, his voice, his very posture were so full of despair that I went after him, to offer spiritual counseling. But all he would accept was a prayer book." The young priest looked down at his untouched cup of tea. "I hope he found in it some form of consolation."

"He must have," said Father Raywood, "because six months later, a check arrived, signed by Christopher Smith. It was for an enormous sum. An enclosed note explained that it was meant as repayment for the prayer book, and requested that the balance be used to feed the needy."

"I was stunned," said Father Danos. "And Father Raywood wasn't at all comfortable with the donation."

The older priest sighed. "It seemed a madly extravagant gesture, and I could not forget how dazed Mr. Smith had seemed that night, when he'd spoken with Andrew. I feared that he might be . . . non compos mentis. If he was suffering from a mental disorder at the time he wrote the check, it would of course be impossible for us to accept his donation. We decided, therefore, to contact him."

Father Danos reached into his cassock pocket and withdrew a small slip of white paper. "The bank upon which the check had been drawn directed us to Havorford House, in Belgravia, where Christopher Smith had been living with his married sister, Lady Felicity Havorford." The younger priest's eyes grew cold, as though the mere mention of the name had conjured unpleasant memories.

"When we visited Lady Havorford," Father Raywood said, "she told us that her brother had left her home in March, shortly after his visit to Saint Joseph's. She said that he was as sane as he'd ever been and that he could do what he liked with his inheritance."

Father Danos's lip curled slightly as he added, "She didn't seem overly concerned by her brother's disappearance."

Father Raywood cleared his throat. "Lady Havorford's answers were not entirely reassuring, but since the funds could not be returned to Mr. Smith directly, we decided to accede to his wishes." He motioned toward the massive stove and the walk-in refrigeration unit. "Thousands would have gone hungry if not for Christopher Smith's generous support of our project."

Julian put his hand out for the slip of paper. "May I have Lady Havorford's address? I'd like to inform her that her brother is in hospital."

While Julian tucked the slip of paper into his wallet, I explained the circumstances under which I'd first met Christopher Smith. The two priests weren't as mystified by Kit's deterioration as I'd expected them to be.

"I sensed that his spirit had been grievously wounded," said Father Danos. "The sort of blow from which one does not easily recover."

"He may have felt that a vow of poverty would help him in some way," Father Raywood commented. "He would not be the first man to seek solace in self-sacrifice."

Julian glanced at his watch. "Nine o'clock," he said. "Not too late to pay a call on Havorford House. I'm certain Lady Havorford will want to know about her brother's condition as soon as possible."

Father Danos began to speak, but Father Raywood cut him off.

"Please let us know when Mr. Smith is able to receive visitors," he said, getting to his feet. "Andrew and I would like to be among the first to wish him well."

Julian slipped into his black leather jacket while I put on my coat and gathered up my shoulder bag and Kit's carryall. Before we left the kitchen, I showed the prayer book to Father Danos, who identified it as the one he'd given to Kit four years earlier. He seemed gratified to see that it had been so well used.

"Father Danos," I said, as we crossed the dining room, "who is Saint Joseph of Cupertino?"

The young priest smiled. "I looked it up after Mr. Smith left. Saint Joseph of Cupertino is the patron saint of aviators. Rather ironic, when you come to think of it."

"Why ironic?" I asked.

"Because Stepney was devastated by the Luftwaffe during the war," he replied. "Saint Joseph's is the only building in the immediate vicinity that survived the blitz. It would be ironic if the church were dedicated to the patron saint of those who nearly destroyed it, don't you agree?"

I nodded absently, remembering Julian's joke about the mad millionaire masquerading as a tramp at Saint Benedict's. It no longer seemed quite so absurd. When Kit Smith had come to Saint Joseph's, he'd been well groomed and well heeled. By the time he reached Saint Benedict's, he'd suffered through four years of abject, self-inflicted poverty.

What had happened on that cold night in February? What had sent Kit to a soup kitchen in Stepney, in search of the patron saint of aviators? What had inspired him to give away his inheritance and trade a fashionable address in Belgravia for a life on the road? What had driven him to make the hard journey that had ended in my graveled drive?

"Ms. Shepherd?" said Father Danos. "Father Bright is waiting for you."

"I'm coming," I said, and followed him up the stairs. When we reached the foyer, I paused to thank the priests for their help, then joined Julian, who stood with his hand on the latch, ready to leave.

As he opened the door, a wind-driven spatter of sleet lashed my face and peppered the foyer's clean floor. A heavy shroud of snow was falling from the black sky, dimming the security floodlights, turning the churchyard and the street beyond into a roiling whirlpool of menacing shadows. I gazed into the darkness, felt an icy finger of slush caress my throat, and froze in the doorway.

"I can't," I said, my heart pounding.

Julian cupped a hand to his ear. "Sorry," he shouted. "Didn't hear you. The wind."

"I c-can't go out there," I faltered, and stepped back into the foyer. "Close the door, Julian. Don't let it in." I could hear my voice trip over into panic as I edged away from the howling wind.

Julian put his shoulder to the door and pushed it shut. "It's pretty nasty out," he said, wiping the sleet from his face. "I left Saint Christopher in Oxford, but we'll be fine on the tube. The station's——" He broke off suddenly and stepped toward me. "Lori, you're trembling."

"Why don't we repair to the vicarage?" Father Raywood, too, was gazing worriedly at me. "It's across the——"

"*I can't,*" I cried, and fled blindly into the church.

17

"Lori?" Julian's voice echoed in the incense-heavy air. "It's just me. The others have gone."

I made no reply, but stood, shivering, before the statue of the Virgin, striking match after match, trying feverishly to light a candle.

"Here, let me." Julian loomed beside me, a moving shadow in the gloom, and I stumbled back, leaving the chained matchbox holder swinging like a pendulum from the wrought-iron candle rack.

A match flared, bright as a star. Julian lit one candle, then another.

"Light them all," I said hoarsely.

"The offering," he said, making a wry face. "I don't think I have enough—"

"I do." I tossed Kit's carryall toward a pew, upended my shoulder bag onto the mosaic floor, and scrabbled for my wallet. "I have enough." I emptied my wallet and began stuffing bills into the offerings box, forcing great wads of them through the narrow slot, gouging my palms and

bruising my knuckles on the wrought iron until Julian
seized my wrists and pulled me into his arms.

I stiffened, struggled frantically, then melted against
him, pressing my face to his leather jacket, burrowing into
him, trying to escape the howling inside my head. He
hushed me with wordless murmurs and gently tightened
his hold until the tension in my body eased and I leaned
against him limply, soothed by the rhythmic rise and fall of
his broad chest, by the scent of incense mingled with the
fragrance of warm leather.

"I'm sorry," he said. "You've been under so much pres-
sure at home. I should never have asked you to come here
tonight."

I tilted my face back to look up at him. "I didn't come
because you asked me. I came because I had to."

He gazed down at me, bewildered. "Why?"

"Because . . ." I leaned my forehead against him briefly,
then stepped away from him to stare out over the empty
pews. "Because Kit's *haunting* me. I can't get him out of
my mind. When I close my eyes, it's his face I see. When I
dream, I dream of him." I ran a hand distractedly through
my disheveled curls. "I've never dreamt of Bill, but I
dream of Kit *every night.*"

Julian's palms came to rest on my shoulders. He steered
me to the high pew where I'd tossed Kit's carryall, sat beside me, and leaned forward, his hands loosely clasped between his knees. "Tell me about your dreams."

"My dreams?" I gave a sobbing laugh. I'd expected Julian
to be dismayed, perhaps disgusted, by my obsession with
someone other than my husband. I hadn't expected him to
ask about my dreams. "They're always the same," I told
him. "Kit's healthy and happy and galloping down the bridle path on a big horse. The horse throws him, and by the
time he hits the ground, he's sick and dressed in rags. He

lands right in front of the cottage, he even watches me through the window, but I don't see him. Then he falls over, holding Anne Somerville's stuffed horse. His hands . . ." I looked down at my bruised knuckles and swallowed hard. "They're black and shriveled, like claws."

Julian nodded slowly, then rose and walked over to gaze up at the Blessed Virgin. He took up the matchbox and began lighting candles, one by one, until all of them were ablaze, their flames like fingers pointing heavenward in the still air. The candles' limpid glow revealed the scattered mess of belongings I'd dumped from my shoulder bag onto the floor. I knelt to gather them up.

"Have you ever been thrown from a horse?" Julian asked.

"I've never even ridden one," I replied.

"But still, you've been thrown." Julian lit the last candle, and knelt to pick up a gold-inlaid fountain pen that had skittered under the candle rack. He rolled it between his fingers, letting the gold catch the candlelight, before handing it to me. "Have you always been wealthy?"

"Are you kidding?" Julian's questions made no sense to me, but I welcomed the distraction from my own turbulent thoughts. "My dad died just after I was born and my mom raised me by herself. We weren't poor, but we weren't even within shouting distance of wealthy."

"But you grew up knowing what it was to do without," Julian observed.

"Not really." I sat back on my heels. "My mom was the one who did without, so that I could have pretty much everything I wanted. When I left my first husband, I had no idea how hard it'd be to start over again from scratch. I had nothing."

"Apart from a fine mind," Julian put in.

"I was too depressed to use it." I retrieved a tortoiseshell brush from under the pew and slipped it into my bag. "Then my mom died and the depression got worse. I had no family left, no real home, and I was barely making ends meet. One night I began toying with the idea of giving my wrists a close shave."

Julian paled. "Dear Lord . . ."

"I didn't do it." I pushed back the sleeves of my cashmere coat and held my unscarred wrists out to him.

"That you considered it is terrible enough." Julian brushed his fingertips across my wrists. "What stopped you?"

I smiled sheepishly, the howling wind forgotten. "A letter from a rich lawyer," I said. "From Bill, my husband, in fact. Little did I know when I set out for his office that night—" I caught my breath and sank back against the pew, dizzied by sudden revelation. It was as if a thousand candles had flickered to life, illuminating memories I'd tucked carefully in the darkest corner of my mind. "That night," I repeated, gazing at a scene only I could see.

"What happened that night?" Julian's voice seemed to come from somewhere up among the banded arches and the redbrick domes.

"The wind was howling." I spoke slowly at first, then faster, as the vision became more vivid. "An April blizzard had blown in. The sleet hurt my face and the streets were covered with slush. I was weak-kneed with hunger, and by the time Bill opened the door, I couldn't feel my toes. If he hadn't opened the door . . ." My voice sank to a whisper. "It could have been me, Julian. Kit could have been me."

I gazed into the middle distance, aware of the chill seeping up from the mosaic floor, of the crushing darkness just beyond the pool of candlelight. I knew how precarious the light was, how quickly the darkness could close in, and I knew, better than most, that it could happen to anyone, anyone at all.

Julian said nothing, but quietly gathered up the rest of my belongings, then drew me up to sit beside him on the hard wooden bench. "Is it any wonder that you dream of Kit instead of Bill?" he said finally. "You and Kit have shared experiences that your husband can never truly understand. Kit was a part of you before he ever stumbled up your drive."

I nodded, acknowledging the truth of Julian's words. Bill had grown up in a world of wealth and privilege. He'd never known what it was to be cold, hungry, and alone in the world. But I had.

"I'd forgotten," I said, half to myself. "I *tried* to forget."

"Evidently it's time to remember," said Julian.

I ran my palms along the sleeves of my cashmere coat and the fine tweed of my custom-tailored trousers. I thought of the overstuffed sofa in my living room and the overstocked pantry in my kitchen. The cottage was a snug nest, a comfortable cocoon in which bad things did not happen. Was it too comfortable, too snug?

I looked up at the face of the Virgin, hovering above us like a pale moon in a starless sky. "My mother used to say that too much comfort is as corrosive to the soul as too little."

"Your mother," Julian observed, "was a wise woman."

And a good woman, I thought, which is more than can be said for her daughter. I bowed my head to avoid the Virgin's gaze.

"Julian," I said, a low-voiced confession, "the first time I saw Kit, I didn't want to touch him. It wasn't my idea to call out the RAF for him, and I wouldn't have visited him at the Radcliffe if someone else hadn't insisted on it. The truth is, I'm not at all like Kit. I've got a shriveled, selfish soul. The only reason I helped Kit was—"

"Because he landed in your front yard." Julian nodded. "Hard to ignore something like that."

"It should be," I said miserably, "but it isn't. I ignore men like Kit all the time. Sometimes I wish they were invisible. They're so . . ." I left the sentence hanging, too ashamed to finish it.

"Repulsive?" Julian suggested. "I agree. They're smelly, ugly, weak—they're totally useless." He put a comforting arm around my shoulders. "I can think of only one good reason why we should bother with them."

I peeped up at him. I knew he was baiting me, and I thought I knew what he wanted me to say. "Because they're human?" I ventured.

"No," said Julian. "Because we are."

In the silence that followed, the vicar's voice seemed to ring out from the empty pulpit: *Let us be thankful for blessings received and eager to share those blessings with others.* I'd been thankful for Dimity's many gifts, but I hadn't done much sharing. I'd used her bounty to create a beautiful world in which no one hungered, froze, or sickened, and I'd turned my back on the sorrows that lay beyond its narrow borders. Perhaps Kit was an angel, I thought, sent to the cottage to shake me out of my smug complacency.

"I've a proposal to make, Lori." Julian crossed his long legs and leaned back. "If, by some miracle, I manage to keep Saint Benedict's going, why don't you come along and lend me a hand once in a while? I could use your help in the kitchen, and the men you meet there will give that shriveled soul of yours a chance to blossom." He inclined his head toward mine. "But it'll still be up to you to do the real work."

"What's that?" I asked.

He raised an admonitory finger. "See to it that no one

who crosses your path is invisible." He extended his hand
and I clasped it to seal the bargain. Far above us, strangely
muted in the church's cavernous reaches, Saint Joseph's
bells began to chime the hour.

"Ten o'clock." Julian pursed his lips. "A bit late to set
out for Belgravia."

"I'm not leaving London before I speak with Kit's sister," I said stubbornly.

Julian shrugged. "Then we'll stay here for the night and
see her first thing tomorrow morning. Father Raywood
said there are cots downstairs, and the kitchen's warm
enough for us to—"

"No." I straightened slightly, but couldn't bring myself
to edge away from the warm circle of his arm. "I don't
think that's such a good idea."

He gave me a playful shake. "Not afraid of spending the
night in a church, are you? Don't worry, you'll be safe
with me."

"But *you* might not be safe with *me*." Exasperation made
me speak without thinking. "Oh, for Pete's sake, Julian,
haven't you figured out yet that I find you attractive?"

"You . . . what?" Julian's look of blank astonishment
told me plainly that the thought had never crossed his
mind. "Don't be ridiculous. You can't possibly find me
attractive."

"Oh yeah?" I retorted. "Well, watch out for lightning
bolts, because if the Virgin can read my mind at this moment, she'll probably fry me."

Julian carefully removed his arm from my shoulders and
folded his hands in his lap. "I'd no idea."

"Now you do." My blush should have outshone the candles. "You know the old saying: I may be married, but I'm
not dead." I glanced heavenward. "Yet."

Julian faced forward, clearly disconcerted. "I could

understand it if you harbored romantic notions about Kit," he reasoned. "Kit's a fine-looking man, but I've got a face like a . . . a . . ."

"A basset hound," I offered.

"Precisely," he agreed, unfazed. "I wouldn't call a basset hound attractive, would you? Unless . . ." He raised a hand to his goatee. "Is it the beard? Perhaps I should shave it off."

"It's not the beard," I said, coloring to my toes. "It's nothing to do with your looks. It's your passion, your tenderness, your humility. You're a good man, Julian, and goodness is tremendously attractive." I snatched a quick breath and thought: In for a penny, in for a pound. "And in case you think I'm being unbearably high-minded, let me just add that you've got a beautiful voice and exquisite hands, and let's face it, Julian, you've got a body to die for."

"Good Lord," Julian said weakly. "Do I?"

I pressed my palms to my burning cheeks. "Take my word for it. It must come from hauling around all those vats of boiled cabbage."

There was a nerve-racking pause, then a gust of laughter that ruffled the candle flames. Julian bent forward, clutching his sides, laughing until tears leaked from the corners of his eyes.

I gave him a very dark look. "You must have a high old time in the confessional, Father Bright."

"I'm sorry," he gasped. "It's just . . . a basset hound . . . hauling vats of cabbage . . ." He gulped for air. "Perhaps I should make an exercise video?" And he was off again, holding his sides and rocking with hilarity.

I folded my arms. "It's not funny," I muttered, feeling more than a bit put out.

"No." He wiped his eyes and took a few slow breaths. "It's not funny. But it's not a mortal sin, either." He shifted sideways, rested his elbow on the pew, and regarded me thoughtfully. "I think I know what this is all about."

I raised a clenched fist. "If you say one word about maternal instinct, I'll clobber you."

"The instinct I'm thinking of isn't *necessarily* maternal," Julian temporized. "I think you miss your husband, Lori. While Bill's been away your natural, God-given appetites have been"—he stroked his goatee meditatively—"temporarily misdirected to another channel."

I ducked my head, still too embarrassed to meet his gaze. "So this is a job for the Army Corps of Engineers, huh?"

"And what safer channel," Julian continued, "than one you know to be absolutely inaccessible."

His words seemed to echo, although he'd spoken softly, and when the last whisper of sound faded, I turned to face him.

"Because you don't have God-given appetites?" I asked.

Something entirely human flickered briefly in the depths of Julian's brown eyes, but he answered without hesitation. "Because I believe, as you do, in the sanctity of marriage." He gazed at me steadily, then put out his hand. "You know you can trust me, Lori, even if you can't trust yourself."

I gazed up at the shadowy planes of his face, the glimmering, dark pools of his eyes, and slowly took his hand in mine. As we sat, fingers entwined, bathed in soft candlelight, I felt warmed from within, not by the fiery flames of passion, but by the unwavering glow of a far deeper and longer-lasting love.

"I do trust you, Julian," I said, resting my head against his shoulder, "but if you think I'm going to spend the night sleeping on a cot in a soup kitchen, you're insane as well as inaccessible."

18

One of the nicest things about being filthy rich and married to a Willis was that I could always get a room at the Flamborough Hotel. In far less time than it took us to cross the frozen tundra between Stepney and Mayfair, Julian and I found ourselves wrapped in luxurious bathrobes, sipping large brandies, and toasting our slippered feet before a fire in the spacious living rooms of the three-bedroom suite assigned to us by the redoubtable Miss Kingsley.

"I can feel my soul corroding," Julian said drowsily.

"Yeah," I murmured. "Ain't it great?"

Julian gave muzzy chuckle. "It makes a change from Saint Benedict's."

"It's the first part of your Christmas present," I told him. "I'll give you the rest as soon as I've sorted out the details."

Julian slouched lazily in his oversized armchair. "If I weren't so sleepy, I'd be intrigued by that comment."

"I'll tell you what intrigues me." I tilted my head to one side and noted distantly that the room appeared to tilt along with it. "Did you notice the way Father Danos practically held his nose every time he mentioned Lady Havorford?"

"Perhaps she has an aversion to clerical garb," Julian suggested. He lifted his head slightly and opened his eyes. "By the way, I've been meaning to ask: where, exactly, are our clothes?"

"They're being cleaned," I replied. "You'll find them hanging in your closet tomorrow morning."

Julian nestled back into his chair. "Delivered by the same elves who provided our pajamas, one presumes."

"Naturally. They're recharging my cell phone, too."

"Clever elves," Julian murmured.

A disturbing thought floated gently through the amber mist enveloping my brain. "What if Lady Havorford isn't home tomorrow morning?"

"She will be," said Julian. "Father Raywood told me she's renowned for her Christmas Eve brunches. Speaking of which, has your husband arrived home yet?"

"My husband," I said, with a deliberateness born of disbelief, "is in Iceland." I'd telephoned the cottage as soon as we'd arrived at the Flamborough and Willis, Sr., had given me an update on Bill's travels. "His plane landed in Reykjavík for refueling this morning and wasn't allowed to take off again because of high winds."

"Oh, Lori"—Julian heaved a sympathetic sigh—"I'm so sorry."

I should have been, too. My family-round-the-hearth fantasy had turned into a family-round-the-world farce. I thought of Bill marooned in Iceland, of unthawed turkeys, unwrapped presents, and unhung wreaths, and began, unaccountably, to giggle.

"Ah, well," I said airily. "Iceland's not too far from the North Pole. Maybe Bill can hitch a ride with Santa Claus."

"No more brandy for you, Ms. Shepherd." Julian put his

Waterford tumbler on the rosewood table beside his chair and yawned hugely. "No more for me, either. If I don't go to bed this minute, I shall fall asleep sitting up."

"You'll regret it if you do," I said. "The beds here are even cushier that the chairs."

"I find that extremely hard to believe," said Julian, "but I'm willing to put it to the test." He pushed himself to his feet. "Good night, Lori."

"Good night, Julian." I watched him amble slowly to his bedroom, finished my drink, and went to mine.

Despite the brandy and the old-cotton softness of the embroidered bedclothes, I found it difficult to fall asleep. I'd telephoned the Radcliffe after I'd spoken with Willis, Sr., half hoping that a Christmas miracle had occurred and that Kit had finally awakened from his coma. But no miracle had taken place. If anything, Kit had weakened slightly. I said a silent prayer for him, pushed the covers aside, and climbed out of bed.

I stood before the window for a time, gazing down at the gusts of snow haloing the street lamps. The glass was too thick, the frame too solid to let in the wind's howl, but I could hear it nonetheless, and no amount of brandy could chase away the chill it sent through my soul.

Somewhere out there, someone like Kit was slowly freezing to death. In a doorway, under a bridge, or in plain sight of shoppers hastening home with armloads of last-minute purchases, someone was cold, hungry, and alone. I pressed my palms to the glass and let the chill course though my body.

I needed the howling wind, needed it to remind me that I was part of a world stretching beyond the snug circle of my family and friends. There was work to be done in that world, and I was blessed beyond all reason with the means to do it.

"Let us see in the poorest among us the face of the Christ Child." I whispered the vicar's words as a promise to Kit, to Julian, and to myself, then turned toward bed.

Julian and I had nearly finished our room-service breakfast the next morning when a knock sounded at the door of the suite.

"Madam?" called a familiar voice. "Limo's ready."

I flew to the door and flung it open. "Paul!" I exclaimed. "I didn't know you were available. I was about to call down for snowshoes."

The gray-haired little man in the navy-blue chauffeur's uniform touched two fingers to his forehead, since he was holding his visored cap in his hand, and executed a formal half-bow. "No need for that, madam. Miss Kingsley said I was to take you round to Belgravia, then whisk you back to the cottage toot sweet." His brow furrowed anxiously. "Your party's still on, isn't it, madam?"

Visions of unthawed turkeys danced through my head, but I smiled bravely and said, "It sure is."

Paul relaxed. "Been looking forward to it, madam. Very kind of you to invite me, I'm sure." He gripped his cap with both hands. "Don't mean to rush you, but the storm's left the city in a bit of shambles, and it may take some time for us to—"

"We're on our way," I said, and called for Julian to drop his toast and grab his jacket.

"Never seen nothing like it," Paul muttered. The window separating driver from client in the long black limousine was never closed when I was Paul's passenger. "Lived in London my whole life, madam, and I've never seen snow like this."

The blizzard had indeed left Paul's beloved birthplace in a bit of a shambles, but it was a peaceful shambles. The storm had forced many businesses to close, thereby reducing the number of harried, list-toting shoppers to near zero. Few pedestrians, it seemed, were willing to clamber over the vast mountain ranges of plowed snow piled at each intersection, and even fewer drivers trailed in the wake of the exhaust-belching snowplows that now ruled London's streets.

As a wealthy residential district, Belgravia received priority treatment from the city's fleet of plows. Paul had little trouble maneuvering the limousine through the snow-tunneled thoroughfares to the gates of Havorford House. While Julian spoke into a gatepost-mounted intercom, requesting an interview with Lady Havorford concerning her brother, I craned my neck to view the mansion Kit had fled on that cold February night four years earlier.

Havorford House was several centuries removed from Stepney's postwar council housing, a rigidly symmetrical Palladian palace in silver-gray stone that rose, gleaming, from the center of a small but exquisite walled garden. A filigreed wrought-iron fence separated the garden from the street, and a half-circular drive curved beneath the mansion's porticoed entryway. If snow fell again that day, it would not fall on Lady Havorford's guests.

Gold glittered everywhere, as if the mansion had been gilded for Christmas. Each tree in the garden was hung with tiny golden lights that bobbed in the breeze like dancing fireflies. Golden baubles dangled from the topiary yews lining the drive, gold mesh bows crowned the gates, and candles burned in every window, before massed groupings of white poinsettias. I gazed at the splendid golden wreath adorning the front door and felt my heart burn with envy. I was willing to bet my handmade Italian boots that Felicity Havorford's Christmas tree didn't list.

"It's perfect," I said dismally.

"Too perfect," Julian noted.

I took what consolation I could from his words, knowing that no one could possibly aim that particular barb at the cottage.

The gate finally swung open and Paul cruised past the topiary yews, coming to a stop beneath the colonnaded porch. Two dark-suited young men trotted out to open the limousine's doors. One of the men escorted Julian and me into the mansion while the other stayed behind to give Paul instructions on parking.

"I'm Budge," said our escort, after Julian and I had handed our coats over to yet another dark-suited young man. "Please, come with me."

Budge led us down a mirror-lined hallway hung with crystal chandeliers to a set of double doors leading to a sumptuous library. As he bowed himself out of the room he informed us that Lady Havorford would be with us shortly.

Once Budge was out of sight, I let loose a pent-up sigh of admiration. The library was unlike any I'd ever seen. Panels of gilded plasterwork, as delicate as the finest embroidery, ornamented the coved ceiling, and a gilded balcony reached by a white-painted spiral staircase gave access to the upper shelves of books. The cream-colored shelves were set in arched niches separated by gold-veined marble pilasters topped with gilded cornices.

A pair of Chippendale chairs and a delicate gilded table sat on one side of the fireplace, facing a sofa upholstered in gold brocade with gilded arms and legs. The floor was covered by a creamy carpet overlaid with a peach-and-gold Aubusson rug, and a wood fire burned merrily in the gold-veined marble hearth. A ponderous mahogany desk set at an angle in the far corner struck the only wrong note in the room.

"Oh, Julian, isn't it magnificent?" I said, hugging Kit's carryall to me as I took in every glittering detail.

"I suppose so." Julian tapped an index finger against his lips and frowned at the Chippendale chairs. "I'm trying, but I can't picture Kit in this setting. Can you?"

I shrugged. "Which Kit? The one I found or the one with the Savile Row tailor?"

"Good point," said Julian.

The double doors opened in concert, as if on invisible strings, and a voice sounded from the mirrored hallway. "The brunch guests will be arriving within the hour, Budge. See to it that the drive is kept clear."

"Very good, my lady."

A woman glided into the room and the double doors closed behind her. She was tall and slender, dressed in a full-skirted, floor-length gown of ivory satin topped with a form-fitting, cropped satin jacket. Her dark brown hair was swept upward in a casual arrangement of soft waves that must have taken hours to perfect. Diamonds glittered on her breast and dripped from her earlobes.

There was no mistaking her identity. She was a good deal older than Kit, but the family resemblance was still strong. Her pale, long-fingered hands were exactly like his. She had the same high cheekbones and curving lips, but her eyes were a faded powder-blue and her expression was curiously lifeless. She seemed more remote standing before us than Kit had lying unconscious in his hospital bed. If Kit's beauty drew people toward him, Lady Havorford's held them at bay.

I noted the similarities and differences, then murmured, "You have Kit's hands."

"Kit?" Lady Havorford regarded me coolly. "A distasteful sobriquet. While you are in my home you will refer to my brother as Christopher. Unless, of course, there's been some mistake——"

"There's no mistake," said Julian, stepping forward. "I'm sorry to be the bearer of bad news, Lady Havorford, but Ki—Christopher is gravely ill. He's at the Radcliffe Infirmary, in Oxford. He's been in a coma for more than a week."

"I see." Lady Havorford motioned for us to sit on the sofa, then glided over to sit gracefully in the chair nearest the fire. Her gaze drifted to Kit's carryall as I placed it on the floor at my feet, but if she recognized it she gave no indication. "Did Christopher ask you to come to me?"

"He wasn't able to," Julian replied.

"Then how did you find me?" she asked.

I gave Julian a quick, puzzled glance. Lady Havorford's questions were beginning to seem somewhat odd. She hadn't asked about the nature of Kit's illness or his prognosis. She hadn't asked how or where Julian and I had come to know her brother or what our relationship was to him. It was hard to tell what was going on behind those powder-blue eyes, but so far she'd betrayed no sign whatsoever of sisterly concern.

"It's rather an involved story, Lady Havorford," Julian told her. "Suffice it to say that Ms. Shepherd and I made certain inquiries on your brother's behalf which led us to Saint Joseph's Church in Stepney. The vicar there led us to you."

A flicker of annoyance crossed Lady Havorford's face, but she said nothing.

"Your brother will need someone to look after him while he convalesces," Julian prodded gently.

"I don't think Christopher would care to be cosseted by me," said Lady Havorford. "He renounced his family four years ago, when he handed over his inheritance to that perversely popish little priest in Stepney."

I opened my mouth to protest, but snapped it shut when Julian's foot nudged mine.

"There are those," he said carefully, "who believe that your brother should be confined for his own protection, once he recovers from his present, physical ailment. Do you agree with them, Lady Havorford?"

I leaned forward, eager for her answer, and watched in fascination as her eyes began to glisten. A moment later, as if of their own accord, two perfect pear-shaped tears rolled down her motionless face.

"My brother may very well be insane," she said evenly, "but then, so might you be, if you'd killed your own father."

19

Lady Havorford surveyed our shocked expressions with cool indifference. "You don't believe me. No one ever does. But my brother knows the truth and so do I."

"Would you be so kind as to share the truth with us?" Julian asked.

"Are you certain you want to hear it?" she returned.

"We are," said Julian.

Lady Havorford carefully blotted her tears with a lace-edged handkerchief drawn from the sleeve of her satin jacket, then rose to her feet. Her gown rustled as she glided to the mahogany desk, where she lifted the receiver of a white telephone. She spoke into it briefly before returning to her chair.

"We shan't be disturbed," she said, adding vaguely, "It will be the first time in ten years that I've left it to my husband to welcome our guests."

I look from her impassive face to the handkerchief twisted tightly in her clenched fists and wondered queasily what she'd say next. I didn't believe for one minute that Kit had killed anyone, much less his own father. Perhaps, I thought, gazing at those white-knuckled hands, it wasn't Kit who was insane, but his sister.

"The curious thing," Lady Havorford mused aloud, "the thing that throws everyone off the scent, is that Christopher grew up adoring Papa. Sir Miles was a hero, you see, a highly decorated member of the most elite corps in Bomber Command."

"Your father was a Pathfinder," I guessed, glancing at the canvas carryall.

Lady Havorford seemed unsurprised by my remark. "You've no doubt heard of the Pathfinder Force lectures Sir Miles gave at Oxford."

"Y-yes," I stammered, as another piece of the puzzle dropped into place. Kit's father had indeed been a university lecturer, just as he'd told Luke Boswell. "We knew he'd given the lectures, but we didn't know what they were about."

A slight frown creased Lady Havorford's smooth brow. "How, then, did you know that my father was a Pathfinder?"

"We didn't," I said, "but . . . here, let me show you what Christopher had with him when he was admitted to the Radcliffe."

I took the water-stained suede pouch from the carryall, teased open the drawstrings, and upended it over the gilded table beside Lady Havorford's chair. As the medals spilled onto the table, she caught her breath, then pursed her lips in a disapproving frown.

"Papa's medals," she said, laying the handkerchief aside. "They were the only things Christopher would accept from the estate, and just look what a mess he's made of them." Her hands hovered briefly over the tangled pile of decorations. Then, with swift, precise movements, she began separating one from another, smoothing the wrinkled ribbons and laying them out in orderly lines. The exercise seemed to stir more memories, for she continued to speak of the distant past.

"We lived in the country when Christopher was small," she said. "He had a horse, called Lancaster, after the first bomber Papa piloted. Christopher would gallop Lancaster along the bridle path, dropping his make-believe bombs neatly on make-believe submarine bases, then dash back to the manor house to tell Papa about his precision-bombing runs."

She paused to examine her display with a critical eye before placing the golden eagle above the other medals, bars, and badges on the table.

"It sounds an idyllic childhood," Julian prompted.

"It was," Lady Havorford agreed. "Then Mother died, and when Papa remarried he sold our country house and we came to live in London." Her voice softened. "It broke Christopher's heart to give up Lancaster, but he never complained. As I said, he adored Papa."

A log fell on the fire, sending up a shower of sparks, and a clamor of voices sounded from the mirrored hallway, but Lady Havorford went on as if there'd been no interruption.

"At school, Christopher never tired of telling his chums of the medals Sir Miles had won," she said. "One day, one of the boys, out of jealousy or spite, pointed out that no campaign medal was ever struck to honor the men of Bomber Command *and for good reasons*. It wasn't until Christopher read history at university that he discovered what those reasons were."

"Area bombing," Julian murmured.

Lady Havorford's eyebrows rose. "You *have* done your research, Father Bright."

Julian turned to me. "It was in the book I borrowed from you, the one from Luke Boswell's shop. During the Second World War, the RAF intentionally bombed civilians, hoping to destroy German morale. No one outside Bomber Command knew much about it until after the war."

"Christopher was horrified to think that Papa's bombs had fallen on schoolyards as well as submarine bases," said Lady Havorford.

"Many people were horrified, once the truth was known," Julian pointed out. "That's why the men of Bomber Command were never awarded a campaign medal."

"But they were soldiers," I said, "and it was war. They were only——" I nearly said, "They were only following orders," but the implications of the phrase silenced me.

"They were doing what needed to be done," Lady Havorford stated flatly. "Christopher, however, saw things differently. He called Papa a monster. He said that Papa was no better than the terrorists whose bombs kill innocent passersby. He moved here, to live with me, and a short time later he left university to work for a friend who owned a stable."

"Did Sir Miles respond to the accusations?" Julian asked.

"He began writing a memoir," said Lady Havorford, "to explain himself to his son." She rose from her chair and returned to the mahogany desk. She stood over it for a moment, gazing down at the blotter, the inkwell, the green-shaded reading lamp, then sat behind it, facing us across a vast expanse of polished wood.

"He compiled most of it at this desk, after long days spent at the Imperial War Museum." She opened a side drawer and withdrew from it a thick sheaf of papers bound with a black ribbon. "Papa worked on his memoir for more than a decade," she continued, placing the manuscript on the blotter, "but Christopher showed no interest in Papa's work. Neither he nor I saw the memoir until . . . after."

"After what?" coaxed Julian.

Lady Havorford folded her hands atop the manuscript's black ribbon. "Four years ago," she said, "Papa was asked to travel to Normandy, to participate in the ceremonies commemorating the fiftieth anniversary of the D-day invasion."

"Another honor for Sir Miles," Julian commented.

"It would have been," Lady Havorford acknowledged. "He was, alas, unable to attend. The D-day ceremonies took place in June, you see, three months after Papa had remembered quite another anniversary." She looked from Julian's face to mine. "Does the thirteenth of February mean anything to you?"

Four years ago, in February, Kit had fled his sister's home to search for the patron saint of aviators. Had he quarreled with his father on the anniversary of a long-forgotten battle? Even as I shook my head, I wondered nervously if Kit had somehow injured his father, then gone to Saint Joseph's, hoping for some kind of absolution.

"On the thirteenth day of February, 1945, my father flew a mission deep into Germany," said Lady Havorford. "As a Pathfinder, he carried a full load of incendiaries to mark the target and set it well ablaze. He fulfilled his mission brilliantly. By the end of the first night's bombing, the glare in the sky above the target could be seen from two hundred miles away.

"By the end of the second night," she continued, "some twenty-five thousand people were dead—twenty-five thousand men, women, and children, residents of the city as well as refugees fleeing from the Russian army, burnt or blasted or suffocated by the firestorm that sucked the oxygen from their lungs." Her hand caressed the manuscript. "The target wasn't a munitions factory or a submarine base. It was a virtually defenseless medieval city renowned for its art and the beauty of its architecture. You may have heard of it. It was called Dresden."

The fire's pleasant crackle seemed to rise to a menacing roar, and the wheezing sighs of sizzling sap sounded eerily like agonized screams. The room's decorative giltwork shimmered as though licked by tongues of flame, but Lady Havorford's eyes were as cold as ice as she raised her hand and pointed to the gilded balcony.

"On the thirteenth day of February," she said, "fifty years after the raid on Dresden, my father hanged himself, just there, above his volumes on military history."

Somewhere beyond the double doors a sweet tenor voice warbled "God Rest Ye Merry, Gentlemen." I thought of Kit, standing in the rain at the end of a weed-grown runway, murmuring prayers to the empty sky, bereft of all comfort and joy.

Lady Havorford's hand came back to rest on the manuscript. "Christopher was here that evening," she said. "He found Papa's body. He also found the letter in which Papa confessed to crimes against humanity and sentenced himself to the proper death for a war criminal."

Julian seemed to wilt beside me, as if the weight of Sir Miles's tragedy had fallen on his own shoulders. "The poor, tormented soul," he murmured.

"My father requires no man's sympathy," said Lady Havorford, her voice filled with disdain. "Sir Miles was a great man tormented by an ungrateful son. Christopher cherished the world my father fought to preserve even as

he condemned the way in which my father fought to preserve it. Papa was a hero. Christopher is a hypocrite as
well as a murderer."

"He's not a murderer," I put in gently. "Your father committed suicide."

"Christopher drove him to it," snapped Lady Havorford.
"Sir Miles never lost a moment's sleep over his part in the
war until Christopher filled his mind with doubt." Her
hands turned to fists atop the memoir. "It was only after
his son lost faith in him that he lost faith in himself."

"Did you accuse your brother of murder?" Julian asked.

"I didn't have to," Lady Havorford replied. "Once he'd
seen the memoir, he knew exactly what he'd done." Her
powder-blue eyes narrowed. "I told him he had no right to
his legacy and he agreed. He should have transmitted his
inheritance to my son, but instead he wasted it on undeserving strangers."

"The money helps a lot of people," I offered.

"A sop to soothe a guilty conscience," said Lady Havorford, softly but venomously. "The first step in his absurd
scheme to redeem himself. Poverty, chastity, good works,
and prayer—sound familiar, Father Bright? Christopher
thought it would cleanse his soul, but I knew better."
She paused to adjust the hang of a diamond earring, adding
almost as an afterthought, "I was relieved when he disappeared, and I have no intention of allowing him to
return."

There was a sudden burst of laughter from the hallway
followed by shouts of *Merry Christmas!* I jumped, startled
by the sound, kicked over the canvas carryall, and sent
Anne Somerville's brown horse tumbling across the
Aubusson rug. With a hasty apology, I scrambled to re-
trieve the scruffy toy.

"Lancaster?" Surprise mingled with distaste in Lady

Havorford's voice. "Don't tell me Christopher's still dragging that nasty old thing around with him."

I looked uncertainly from her to the patched and faded toy. "Lancaster?"

"Christopher named it after his horse," Lady Havorford explained.

I stood, the small horse cradled in my hands. "Lancaster belongs to Kit?"

"He's had it since he was a boy," said Lady Havorford. "A neighbor woman made it for him. Yet another sympathetic soul. She lived in a cottage at the end of our bridle path."

I felt my knees wobble slightly as I looked down at the well-loved little horse. "What was the neighbor woman's name?"

"Westwood," said Lady Havorford. "Miss Dimity Westwood."

20

A bell tolled in the furthest recesses of my mind, and I was instantly transported to my living room, where the Pym sisters sat, describing their fleeting encounter with Kit Smith.

It was rather eerie, to be honest. He reminded us so strongly . . .

. . . of poor Robert Anscombe, who died so long ago. . . .

"Y-your maiden name, Lady Havorford," I managed, returning shakily to the present moment. "Was it, by any chance, Anscombe?"

"Originally, yes," she replied. "It later became Anscombe-Smith. My stepmother insisted on joining her name to ours when she married Papa."

I looked at Julian and gave a short, incredulous laugh. "Christopher Anscombe-Smith," I said. "Kit Smith. Smitty." When he didn't respond, I took a step toward him. "Kit grew up at Anscombe Manor, Julian. That's how he knew about the bridle path. *He grew up next door to Dimity.*"

Lady Havorford favored me with a polite, incurious stare.

"I don't pretend to know what you're talking about"—she held up her hand for silence—"nor do I care. I have told you the truth about my brother. It is a matter of indifference to me whether you believe it or not. I must now attend to my guests. If you'll excuse me . . ."

"Lady Havorford," Julian said urgently, "you must have loved your brother once. If you search your heart, you'll find your love for him still lives, in spite of everything. Won't you please give me a message to bring to him? You may not have another chance."

Lady Havorford floated to her feet and gazed down at Julian imperiously. "You may bring a message to my brother, Father Bright. You may tell him that he will never redeem himself in my eyes, and that I hope he rots in hell."

Lady Havorford smoothed her dress and glided toward the hallway, her beautiful head erect, her satin gown rippling luxuriously as she moved. When the double doors had closed behind her, I saw that Julian had crossed to the mahogany desk.

"Julian," I said, "Budge'll be here in a minute, to kick us out."

"I doubt it." He untied the black ribbon and took up the manuscript. "Lady Havorford wouldn't have left us alone with her father's memoir unless she wanted us to see it." He scanned the topmost sheet, set it aside, and began leafing through the rest of the pages. Suddenly he clutched the sheaf of papers to his chest and looked up at the gilded balcony, his face etched in pain.

"Julian?" I said, hastening to his side. "What is it? What's wrong?"

He pointed to the page he'd set aside. "Read the epigraph Sir Miles chose."

The short quotation was written in a crabbed hand on an unlined and unnumbered sheet of paper:

As soon as men decide that all means are permitted to fight an evil, then their good becomes indistinguishable from the evil that they set out to destroy.
                                    —Christopher Dawson,
                                       The Judgment of Nations (1942)

I looked up at Julian. "It sounds like something Kit might have said to him."

"I hope to God it wasn't," Julian said heavily. "Here, look at the next page."

He handed me a photocopy of a photograph. It was an abstract black-and-white composition, blurred splashes and pinpoints of light against a grainy gray background. The caption, written below the photograph in the same crabbed hand as in the epigraph, identified it as *The first RAF raid on Hamburg, 24 July 1943. Photoflash of city center.*

"It's the firestorm in Hamburg," Julian explained, "as seen from the belly of a bomber. There were pictures like it in the book I borrowed from you. The dots are incendiary bombs. The blurs are where fires are already raging." He placed the rest of the manuscript on the desk. "Turn to the next page and go on turning."

There was no narrative text in Sir Miles's memoir. Instead, each page contained a single photograph, photocopied, no doubt, during the long days he'd spent at the Imperial War Museum.

Some of the photographs were like the first, taken from bombers as they flew over a burning city, but most depicted more readily recognizable scenes: charred bodies, sobbing women, smoking ruins. The captions below the ruins conjured their own haunting visions: *Maternity Hospital, Berlin; Holy Ghost Church, Munich; Refugee Center, Dresden,* and on and on, for more than five hundred pages. I flipped from image to image and finally turned away, unwilling to look further.

"It's not a memoir," I said. "It's a nightmare."

"It's a self-portrait," said Julian, "meant to explain himself to his son."

"What kind of man would leave something like that to his son?" I asked. "It's hellish."

"Imagine how much more hellish it would be to carry those pictures around in your head," said Julian, "to see them in your dreams and in every waking moment of your life—and know you'd had a part in creating them." He walked aimlessly to the middle of the room, pressing his fingers to his temples, as though to drive the obscene images from his mind.

I tapped the pages of the manuscript together, retied the ribbon, and placed them on the blotter, where Lady Havorford had left them. "Do you think Sir Miles was a monster?"

"He was a man of conscience, asked to do unconscionable things." Julian's hands dropped to his sides as he looked toward the gilded table. "His medals must have stabbed at him like a crown of thorns. While his children bragged about his bravery, he brooded over the children he'd destroyed. I've seen it before," he went on, "in the old soldiers who end up at Saint Benedict's after years of trying to erase their memories with drugs or drink."

I thought of the two vagrants, Rupert's mates, who'd saluted me in Preacher's Lane. "What do you do for them?"

"I feed them, listen to them, remind them that God loves them. Sometimes they believe me. Sometimes . . ."

He shrugged helplessly. "I can't condone suicide, but I also can't help wondering how a decent man could live with himself after leading the raid on Dresden." His head snapped up and he glared at the balcony, his eyes glazed with angry tears. "But where could Sir Miles look for help? He was a hero. How can a hero admit to doubt and self-disgust? How can a man who'd done what he'd done believe in the promise of salvation?"

Julian swiped a hand across his eyes, then strode to the gilded table, where he bent to collect Sir Miles's medals and return them to the water-stained suede pouch. I tucked Lancaster into the canvas carryall and stood before the fire, trying to think of something comforting to say.

"I don't believe that Kit drove his father to suicide," I said finally. "I think Sir Miles was on his way there long before Kit confronted him. It's like you said—Sir Miles carried those pictures around in his head. His memories killed him, not Kit."

"What we believe is immaterial," said Julian. "It's what Kit believes that matters. Kit believes himself responsible for his father's madness and death. Sir Miles left his son a legacy of despair." He thrust the suede pouch into the carryall and zipped it shut, as if he never wanted to see the medals again.

I ran a hand through my hair, wishing I could do something to ease the anguish I saw in Julian's eyes. "Sir Miles is beyond our help," I said, "and Lady Havorford doesn't want it. But we can still help Kit."

He took a steadying breath, the straightened his shoulders and nodded toward the double doors. "Come, old friend. It's time we were going home."

"Home," I murmured. I gazed slowly around the perfect bijou of a room and saw grim shadows hovering in every corner. My cottage, with its tilted tree and half-hung decorations, had never seemed so sweet.

The sensible majority of the British population had elected to ride out the storm in the comfort of their own homes. Apart from the inevitable semis, a cadre of emergency vehicles, and a few dozen intrepid fools like ourselves, traffic on the major motorways was nonexistent.

It was no longer snowing, but Paul was forced to drive cautiously, nonetheless. The M40 to Oxford, reduced by the storm to one lane in each direction, was a hazardous maze of abandoned cars and jackknifed trailers made even more challenging by an unpredictable gusting wind that rocked the limo and reduced visibility, on occasion, from yards to inches.

Julian had said nothing since we'd left Havorford House. The depression that had settled over him in the library hung between us like a gray shroud, and I didn't know how to lift it. The questions he'd asked, about decent men and war, seemed unanswerable.

Sighing, I reached for the hamper Miss Kingsley had sent along to keep starvation at bay if we were stranded. In it I discovered three Cornish game hens, two bottles of claret, and assorted side dishes, all of which looked a good deal more appetizing than anything I'd be able to offer my guests. Will and Rob might be content to suck on frozen drumsticks, but I doubted that Bill's English relatives would be so easily satisfied. With a soft groan, I looked out at the blowing snow, wondering what my father would make of my half-baked festivities.

"Worrying about your party?" Julian asked.

"Yeah," I admitted sheepishly, glad of any excuse to get

him talking. "Seems pretty trivial, after what we've learned today."

"Christmas traditions aren't trivial," he asserted. "They brighten the darkest months of the year."

"It sure doesn't feel like Christmas," I said, closing the hamper. "I don't know about you, but my head's so filled with war and suffering that I'm finding it a little hard to believe in Santa." No sooner had I said the words than I saw, as clearly as I'd seen the pictures in Sir Miles's memoir, the photograph of my father standing in the ruins of Berlin. I put the hamper on the floor and turned the image over in my mind. "Did I ever tell you that my father was a soldier?"

"No," said Julian. "You never mentioned it."

"He landed at Omaha Beach," I said, "and fought all the way to Berlin. There's a photograph of him . . ." I looked out at the snow-blurred landscape and saw instead the snow-covered ruins of a war-ravaged city, frozen in grainy black-and-white. "It's Christmas in Berlin, just after the war. He's in his GI uniform and he's handing out presents to a bunch of German kids. Nothing fancy, just chocolate bars and socks and stuff like that. But the looks on the kids' faces—it's like he's giving them the best presents they've ever had."

"It sounds as though they had no trouble believing in Santa," said Julian.

"That's what I'm getting at." I could almost hear the children's laughter as my father filled their hands. "See, Julian, I think that's what a decent man does, after a war. He tries to build a decent world. He doesn't brag or brood. He grabs a sackful of candy and hands it out to his enemy's kids. He helps them believe in Santa Claus again." I rubbed the tip of my nose, embarrassed by my earnestness. "It's not like starting the United Nations, but—"

"But a decent world is built upon small acts of kindness." Julian gazed down at the canvas carryall. "It's something Kit would understand."

"That's right," I said eagerly. "Kit didn't give in to despair. His father may have left him a dark legacy, but Kit chose to light a candle. He lit candles everywhere he went, through acts of kindness large and small."

Julian hesitated, then pulled the carryall into his lap and opened the side pocket. "Such as helping a grieving widow," he said, pulling out the braided loop of straw. "Or closing a dangerous asylum." He held the Heathermoor ID out to me.

I looked down at Kit's wild hair and his gentle, intelligent eyes. "Or using your inheritance to feed the hungry."

Julian paused before adding gruffly, "Or risking your life to save someone else's."

I heard the note of self-reproach in his voice and frowned at him. "Or struggling to keep a hostel open," I stated firmly, "to help the kind of men selfish idiots like me would prefer to ignore."

A slow, sweet smile crept across his face. "Or seeing goodness where an envious fool like me chose to see madness."

I lifted an eyebrow. "I guess Kit wouldn't want us to be depressed about all of that, huh?"

"I'm certain it's the last thing he'd want." Julian tucked the braided straw and the Heathermoor ID into the carryall, placed it on the floor, and swung sideways to face me. "We'll drink his health on Christmas Eve and pray for him on Christmas morning. We'll fill the darkness with light, Lori. That's what Kit would want us to do."

"I suppose that's what Christmas is all about, really," I said. "A child bringing the light of hope to a dark world."

"Very prettily said, madam," Paul piped up from the

front seat. "But don't let's forget presents. Christmas wouldn't be Christmas without presents, now, would it?"

I grinned at him in the rearview mirror. "No, Paul, it certainly wouldn't. I hope you like what Bill and I got for you."

"For me?" Paul's eyes lit with pleasant anticipation. "Oh, madam, you shouldn't have. . . ."

His response, as traditional as carols on Christmas morning, banished the last vestiges of gloom from the limo, and triggered a chain of reminiscences that kept us smiling all the way to Oxford. There would be time to ponder war's myriad tragedies another day, I told myself. Today, hope reigned supreme.

21

I urged Julian to come to my party—such as it was—but he wanted to spend Christmas Eve with his flock, so we dropped him off in Oxford. It was hard to say good-bye to him, but I managed it, without a single tear. He promised to look in on Kit, and I renewed my vow to return to Saint Benedict's as soon as the holidays were over. As he waved to us, surrounded by his scruffy crew on the crumbling doorstep of his decrepit hostel, I caught a glimpse of heaven in his face. I wondered if the bishop knew what a wise decision he'd made when he'd banished his gadfly assistant to live and work among outcasts. And I wondered if Kit would ever know how grateful I was to him for leading me to Julian.

Paul fled the low-rent district as if the hounds of hell were nipping at his tires, and he didn't really relax until we were on the way to Finch. A dusky gloom was settling in by the time we reached the village, and the square seemed curiously deserted. Peacock's pub was dark, the lights were

out in Sally Pyne's tearoom, and a CLOSED sign was hanging on the Emporium's front door.

"Great," I moaned, burying my face in my hands. "Everyone's at the cottage but me and Bill. What am I going to do,
Paul? All I've got to offer them is a burnt gingerbread."

"I shouldn't worry, madam," Paul soothed. "It's a giving
spirit that counts, isn't it?"

"Yeah, right," I muttered, wondering how far I could
stretch three Cornish game hens.

As we passed the mouth of the drive leading to Anscombe Manor, a line of vehicles came into view, parked
end to end along the lane leading to the cottage—the
Hodges' farm truck, the Pym sisters' antiquated "motor,"
Nell's sleigh, Mr. Barlow's snowplow, and at least ten out-
of-county cars that had somehow made it through the
storm intact. Someone had had the foresight to leave
enough room in my driveway for the limo, but no one had
prepared me for the sight that met my eyes when Paul
turned into the drive.

It was as if the cottage had collided with a gaudy carnival
ride. A manically blinking rainbow of lights outlined the
slate roof, the chimney, and the windows; tinselly garlands
dripped from the lilacs' bare branches; and a flock of mu-
tant papier-mâché robins had come to roost on the trellis
framing the front door. A pair of the Peacocks' glowing
choirboys flanked the living room's bow window, and
a row of their three-foot plastic candy-canes stood like a
striped stockade just inside the beech hedge. Sally Pyne's
disembodied Santa heads leered from every window, and
a sinister snowman stood beside the flagstone path, wearing a bicycle helmet, a pair of wraparound sunglasses, and
a wicked grin of coal. The display was garish, tasteless, as
far from perfect as it could ever hope to be—and absolutely glorious.

The windows were ablaze with light, and the stone walls seemed to vibrate with the rumble of a dozen conversations. As I emerged from the limo, the front door flew open and people streamed out into the snow. First came Emma Harris, then Derek, Nell, and—

"Peter!" I exclaimed, as Derek's elusive eighteen-year-old son approached me. "I thought you were paddling up the Amazon."

"I paddled home for the holidays instead," he told me. "Shocked the socks off Dad."

"I'll bet you did," I said, giving him a hug.

After that, I lost track of the hugs given and received. Bill's English relatives had driven in from all corners of the sceptered isle, Miss Kingsley had come up from London, Luke Boswell had made the trip from Oxford, and when I heard a booming voice call out "Merry frigging Christmas, Shepherd!" I knew that at least one plane from America had landed safely at Heathrow.

"Stan!" I cried, as I spotted Dr. Stanford J. Finderman, my plainspoken former boss, standing in the doorway. "You made it!"

"Think I'd miss a free meal?" Stan thundered.

"A m-meal?" I stammered, blushing.

"Get inside, will ya, Shepherd?" Stan bellowed. "I'm freezing my heinie off."

Helpful hands pulled me through the doorway, tugged Kit's carryall from my grasp and the coat from my shoulders, and pushed me into the dining room, where I saw, to my utter amazement, a buffet meal lavish enough to keep a minor nation going for a month.

The table trembled beneath the weight of roast turkey and goose, smoked ham and fine fat sausages, relishes and vegetables, mince pies, and an enormous cut-glass bowl of potent-looking punch. As I stood there, too stunned to think of anything to say, Bill's aunt Anthea thrust a wedge of fruitcake into my hand—not the dry-as-dust variety with the nasty Day-Glo fruit, but the mouthwatering, ninety-proof real thing, aged in stout and chockablock with plump sultanas.

"Either close your mouth or fill it," Anthea ordered.

I chose the latter course, and was still relishing my first bite when Sally Pyne emerged from the kitchen, wrapped in a red apron and carrying a gravy boat.

"Welcome home," she called, setting the gravy boat beside the turkey. "I hope you don't mind me working in your kitchen, Lori," she added, elbowing her way across the room. "When I saw your pantry the other day, I thought what a shame it would be to let such a lovely lot of good food go to waste."

"When did you see my pantry?" I asked, mystified.

"The other day, when you were off in Oxford," Sally replied. "I closed the tea shop and came out here to lend William a hand. You don't think I'd leave him to look after the twins on his own, do you?"

I shot a glance at my father-in-law, who was innocently employing a nutcracker over a mound of filberts, and thought, *You sneaky devil.* I'd often wondered how he managed to look so dapper after a day with Will and Rob. Now I knew.

"Where are my boys?" I shouted above the dining room's din.

"In here, Lori," called a voice from the hallway.

"Francesca?" I dropped the wedge of fruitcake on the table and fought my way to the hall. "Is that you?"

"Adrian seems to think so," my nanny replied.

"I'm sure of it," added her fiancé. "Francesca couldn't possibly be anyone but herself."

I gazed in jubilation at the pair, who were holding a twin

apiece, and tried to seize both of my sons at once, putting a severe strain on my back muscles as well as the boys' patience. Will and Rob were happy to see their long-lost mummy, but not happy enough to put up with being crushed.

"When did you get back from Italy?" I asked, letting Will return to Adrian's arms.

"Yesterday afternoon, before the snowstorm hit," said Adrian. He lowered his voice and leaned closer to me. "When we got here we found Sally Pyne waiting on William hand and foot, while two other local widows were in the kitchen, feeding your sons and ransacking your scullery."

"Three widows at his beck and call," I muttered. "The sly old fox."

"Lori," Emma said excitedly, grabbing me by the arm. "I've finished the computer search on the military decorations. You won't believe the name that came up."

"Yes, Emma, I will." I handed Rob back to Francesca and pulled Emma aside, but before I could tell her about my journey to London, someone took me by the shoulders, turned me around, and planted a hearty kiss directly on my lips.

"G-Gerald," I managed, somewhat breathlessly, falling back a step to gaze up at Bill's devastatingly handsome English cousin.

"Merry Christmas, Lori," said Gerald, grinning broadly. "Kind of you to be so generous with the mistletoe. Lucy and I have been putting it to good use."

"Marriage suits you," I said, my lips still tingling. "Where is Lucy, anyway?"

"In the living room, keeping an eye on Uncle Williston," Gerald told me.

"Uncle Williston's here?" I said, clapping my hands in

delight. Uncle Williston was the most eccentric member
of the Willis clan by a factor beyond calculation. "What's
he wearing?"

"See for yourself." Gerald stood aside and motioned for
me to proceed him into the living room.

The living room was as congested as the dining room,
but Uncle Williston stood out in any crowd. He occupied
Bill's favorite armchair, splendidly arrayed in a green brocade tailcoat, green satin breeches, white stockings, and
gold-buckled, square-toed shoes. Nell Harris sat on a
footstool beside him, with Bertie on her knee, surveying
Uncle Williston's lacy shirtfront with a look of profound
satisfaction.

To one side of the hearth stood Luke Boswell, his thumbs
hooked in a pair of neon-red suspenders, and Stan Finderman, red-faced and quaffing a cup of punch. Stan had
no trouble making himself heard above the clamor: the
subject of their animated discussion was, predictably, rare
books.

Everywhere I looked, I saw familiar faces: Theodore
and Lilian Bunting, Chris and Dick Peacock, Peggy Kitchen
and Jasper Taxman, George Wetherhead and Able Farnham, Mr. Barlow and Miranda Morrow, the Hodges and
the Pyms, talking, laughing, eating, and sipping punch.

One face eluded me, however: the face belonging to
the man in the Father Christmas suit, who stooped before
the listing Christmas tree, arranging beautifully wrapped
packages. Was it Aunt Anthea's husband, I wondered,
eyeing the broad shoulders, or had Willis, Sr., hired a
professional to stand in for Bill? I edged closer to him,
exchanging greetings with all and sundry as I went, and
as I came within arm's reach, he straightened from his
crouch.

"Merry Christmas," I said brightly.

"Ho ho ho!" he replied, and before I could identify the voice, the jolly old elf swung around, yanked off his beard, and swept me into a back-bending, full-contact kiss that first silenced the room, then brought shouts of approval from the assembled throng.

"Bill!" I gasped when he finally released me. "I thought you were in Iceland."

"Hitched a ride with Santa," he said.

"God bless Rudolph," I murmured fervently, and pulled my husband to me for another mistletoe moment. Absence doesn't make the heart alone grow fonder. I could feel my toes curl as Bill's embrace tweaked each and every one of my God-given appetites.

It was hardly the time to indulge them, however. Lilian Bunting, worried by her cast members' frequent trips to the punch bowl, asked us to help her gather her flock and pack them off to the schoolhouse, where the Nativity play was due to start in one hour's time.

Willis, Sr., elected to ride to the village in Nell's sleigh, and as Bill and I stood on the doorstep, waving them off, I had a sudden flash of inspiration.

"I've just thought of another Christmas present," I said.

Bill enfolded me in his Father Christmas cape. "I've already got everything I want."

I leaned against him, savoring the familiar contours of his body, and decided not to tell him that the present I'd thought of wasn't meant for him. "I've missed you so much," I murmured.

"Not half as much as I've missed you." He kissed the top of my head. "Father told me why you went to London. Did you find the answers you wanted?"

"I found answers I didn't know I was looking for." I

raised my head from his chest to look toward the lilac bushes, to the place where I'd first seen Kit Smith. "I'll tell you all about it later. Right now, we have a job to do."

"What's that?" Bill asked.

"Lilian's got the cast and crew together," I told him. "It's up to us to supply the audience."

22

Finch, that night, outshone even my cottage. Electric candles brightened every window and strings of fairy lights outlined each roof, crept from tree to tree around the square, and graced the holly bushes encircling the war memorial. Saint George's Lane was jammed with cars, and bright-eyed revelers trundled between the pub and the schoolhouse doors, where Emma stood, selling tickets and handing out programs.

"How's Lilian holding up?" I asked, when Bill and I reached the doorstep.

"Nerves of steel," Emma replied. "It's Peggy Kitchen who's the basket case. She can't find her beard."

"Beard?" Bill's eyebrows shot up. "Is there something I should know about Peggy before we go inside?"

"You'll find out soon enough, O absent one," I said, and hauled him into the schoolhouse.

Lilian's newfound air of authority had brought an end to the chaos that had reigned during rehearsals. The folding chairs had been arranged in neat rows on either side of a

central aisle, blue velvet drapes spangled with tinfoil stars
had been hung to conceal the stage, and all traces of paint,
sawdust, and sewing detritus had been swept away.

Bill and I found two empty seats in the back corner of
the schoolroom, near Mr. Barlow, who hovered over a
wire-covered lighting board the twins found utterly en-
trancing. While we wrestled with our inquisitive sons,
Dick Peacock pounded out carols on the upright piano, ac-
companied by a chorus of anxious whispers and muttered
deprecations coming from the dressing areas on either
side of the stage.

By the time six o'clock rolled around, every folding
chair had been filled and at least twenty members of the
audience were sitting on windowsills or standing in the
back of the room. When Lilian emerged from the ladies'
dressing area and signaled for Dick Peacock to stop playing, she looked well pleased.

"Welcome," she said, standing before the stage, "and
thank you for taking time from your own private celebrations to share this joyful evening with us. Our play has
rather a special meaning for us this year, as the proceeds
will be donated to Saint Benedict's Hostel for Transient
Men in Oxford." She looked toward me and smiled. "Lori?
Would you care to say a few words?"

I stood, with Will wriggling in my arms, and flushed as
every head turned in my direction.

"I don't think anyone here expected to have anything to
do with a place like Saint Benedict's this Christmas." I
smiled wryly. "I certainly didn't. When Kit Smith showed
up on my doorstep, I was more concerned about head lice
than about his well-being. But I've learned a thing or two
since then. We all have, thanks to Kit."

I shifted Will to my other hip before continuing.

"Kit's arrival in Finch challenged all of us to be bigger

and better than we thought we could be. And we managed, after a few false starts, to meet the challenge. I've never been prouder of my village than I am tonight. Thank you for opening your hands and hearts to Kit Smith and the men of Saint Benedict's."

My words were greeted by dead silence, broken suddenly by vigorous applause. Lilian waited for it to die down before taking the floor once again.

"If it is more blessed to give than to receive," she said, "then it is we who owe Mr. Smith a vote of thanks. Those of you who would care to increase your donation to such a worthy cause may do so on the way out." She paused. "And now, ladies and gentlemen, our play."

Lilian took her seat in the front row, the vicar took his place behind the lectern to one side of the stage, the lights dimmed, and an anticipatory hush fell over the schoolhouse.

"And it came to pass in those days, that there went out a decree from Caesar Augustus, that all the world should be taxed. . . ."

The vicar's pleasant, sonorous voice had its usual soporific effect—the moment he began to speak, the twins stopped squirming. As their heads drooped and they curled sleepily in their travel cots, I wondered fleetingly if Theodore Bunting would be available to read bedtime stories to them for the next five or so years.

"And Joseph also went up from Galilee, out of the city of Nazareth. . . ."

The blue velvet curtains parted jerkily and a spotlight picked out Nell Harris and Willis, Sr., at center stage, standing before the plywood facade of an inn with its door determinedly shut.

The tableau was unexpectedly moving. Nell sat on a moth-eaten vaulting horse, her hands on her swollen belly, her head turned slightly to one side. Her expression, a poignant mixture of patience and disappointment, was heartrending, and Willis, Sr., was equally effective. He stood, humbly clad in sandals and a dusty brown caftan, with one hand on Nell's shoulder and the other pointing the way to the stable, where they would find shelter . . .

". . . because there was no room for them in the inn." The vicar paused, the spotlight faded, and the curtains jerked shut to a ripple of applause. Dick Peacock struck up a chorus of "Angels We Have Heard on High" that nearly succeeded in drowning out the thumps and grumbles coming from behind the curtain as the scenery was shifted.

"Your father's done you proud," I whispered to Bill.

"Remind me to tell him so when we get home," he whispered back.

"I will," I assured him.

"And there were in the same country shepherds abiding in the field," intoned the vicar, "keeping watch over their flock by night."

The curtains opened a couple of feet and the spotlight fell lopsidedly on a sheep munching contentedly on a flake of alfalfa hay. The sheep won an instant round of applause.

An offstage voice whispered urgently, *"Pull harder!"* and the curtains flew apart. The spotlight widened to illuminate George Wetherhead and Able Farnham, dressed in bathrobes, with cord-bound dish towels draped artfully over their heads. Each clutched a sturdy shepherd's crook— Lilian's clever solution to the pair's mobility problems. Between them, and slightly upstage of the sheep, stood an exceptionally corpulent palm tree, silhouetted against a backdrop of bilious green hills.

"And, lo, the angel of the Lord came upon them," read the vicar, "and the glory of the Lord shone round about them: and they were sore afraid."

Mr. Barlow pushed a lever and a second spotlight picked out Miranda Morrow, Finch's freckle-faced, wholesome-looking witch, rising from the palm tree's uppermost fronds. Miranda's strawberry-blond hair had been crimped to form a berserk halo, and the wings on her back, though white, seemed more suitable to a bat than to an angel.

Able Farnham and George Wetherhead did a very good job of miming fear without budging one inch from their original, safely balanced positions. The sheep seemed unimpressed.

"And the angel said unto them . . ." The vicar paused.

"Fear not," called Miranda Morrow, spreading her arms wide, "for behold, I bring you good tidings of great joy, which shall be to all people. For unto you is born this day in the city of David a Savior, which is Christ the Lord. . . ."

I'd heard the words a hundred times before, but tears pricked my eyes nonetheless, and as the play continued, I was swept up in its magic. Nothing—not even the sight of Peggy Kitchen in a jury-rigged false beard—could rob the ancient tale of its mystery and power. I looked from Piero Hodge's tiny bare foot, kicking vigorously in the manger, to Will and Rob, sound asleep in their cots, and felt joy rise within me. All children are children of light, I thought. All children bring hope to the world.

The players were greeted with tumultuous applause when they lined up for their bows, and the roof nearly came off of the schoolhouse when Willis, Sr., drew Lilian from her chair to stand beside him at center stage. Dick Peacock harnessed the energy by leading everyone—cast, crew, and audience alike—in an exhilarating chorus of "Hark, the Herald Angels Sing" and brought the evening to a close with a single verse of "Silent Night."

Will and Rob had been subjected to more than enough excitement for one day, so Bill and I sent them home with Francesca before accompanying our out-of-town guests to Anscombe Manor. With typical fickleness, the winter wind had changed from bitter to balmy during the course of the play, and the sky had begun to clear. By the time we reached the manor house, a single star shown brightly above the stable, where young Christopher Anscombe had spent the happiest days of his childhood.

"You and I should learn to ride," I said to Bill, as we tramped through the snow to the manor house's courtyard entrance. "The boys too, when they're old enough."

"Me, on a horse?" Bill leered at me with mock suspicion. "After my insurance, eh?"

I laughed. "It's someone else's insurance I'm thinking of. I'll fill you in later."

Emma and Derek had prepared a feast as bountiful as the one my neighbors had laid on at the cottage. The great hall was hung with greenery and lit with candles, and when the play's cast arrived to celebrate their triumph, they were greeted with a rousing cheer. Bill and I drank from the wassail bowl, sampled the Christmas pudding, and mingled happily before bidding our guests good night and heading home.

"Do I have you to thank for bringing Christmas to the cottage?" I asked, as we pulled into the drive.

"Not guilty," Bill proclaimed, eyeing the deformed robins clinging to the trellis. "Father let it be known that you were off helping Kit Smith and the villagers took it from there. They were at it all night in the kitchen, and they spent all morning desecrating—er, I mean, *decorating*—the cottage."

"It's not what I had planned." I thought of the hard work and the enormous kindness that had gone into the appalling display, and sighed happily. "It's much better."

We linked arms as we strolled up the snow-covered flagstone path, and when we reached the doorway, I looked hesitantly up at my husband.

"Bill," I said, "I know you want to hear about the amazing journey I've been on, but . . . there's someone else I need to talk to first."

Bill tapped his wristwatch. "I'll give you a half hour," he said. "Then I'm coming in after you." He bent down to kiss me soundly before adding, "Tell Dimity that Father Christmas sends his best."

Reginald was waiting for me in the study. My pink bunny sat on the ottoman, backlit by the fire in the hearth, gazing expectantly at the doorway as I entered the room. I placed Kit's carryall beside him, took Aunt Dimity's blue journal from its place on the bookshelves, and sat in the tall leather armchair.

"I'm glad you're here, Reg," I said. "There's someone I'd like you to meet." I unzipped the carryall and took out the little brown horse, then opened the blue journal and leaned back. "His name's Lancaster. I'm pretty sure you're cousins."

I looked down at the blue journal and saw a single word appear on the page in Aunt Dimity's old-fashioned copperplate.

Christopher.

"That's right," I said. "Kit Smith, the tramp, is Christopher Anscombe, the boy who used to ride over from Anscombe Manor along the bridle path."

We never called him Kit. But I should have known. Sir Miles Anscombe, the Pathfinder badge . . . I should have known.

"You were thinking in a completely different direction," I told her. "You were trying to remember an airman you'd met on a base up in Lincolnshire, not a little boy who grew up next door."

What happened to Christopher? How did such a shining child end up living as a tramp?

I ran a thumb along Lancaster's tangled mane, then set him gently beside Reginald. "It has to do with his father."

But Sir Miles was a

"A hero," I broke in. "Yes, I know. He was a hero who bombed schoolhouses and churches, who killed mothers and babies and old men. And he did it all because he wanted to make the world a better place for his own children. He used evil to fight evil, and in the end he came to believe that he was evil. Dimity . . ." I searched for a way to soften the blow, but found none. "Four years ago, Sir Miles Anscombe committed suicide."

A sigh seemed to drift through the room, ruffling the fire's bright flames. *So he finally succeeded.*

I stared down at the page, blinking stupidly. "W-what?"

Sir Miles finally succeeded in killing himself. He'd tried several times before, at Anscombe Manor. That's why his second wife decided to sell the place and move the family to London. She thought a change of setting would help Sir Miles settle down, but there's only so much one can do for a man who's bent on self-destruction.

I ran a hand through my already disheveled curls and thought a moment. "Did the children know why they moved to London?"

Felicity did. She was old enough to be told the truth, but Christopher was far too young.

"Do you think Kit ever knew about his father's suicide attempts?" I asked.

I doubt the topic was discussed at dinner. The family was very careful of Sir Miles's reputation. But I knew the moment he showed me his dreadful memoir that he was as potty as a tin of shrimp.

I sat bolt upright. "When did he show you his memoir?"

Years ago, before he left Anscombe Manor. When he told me that he planned to leave those horrid pictures to his son, I nearly struck him.

I gazed at Reginald, who seemed to nod in the flickering firelight, as if to confirm my growing suspicions. "Did Felicity get along with Christopher?"

She told everyone who'd listen that she loved her baby brother to distraction, but I was never taken in. She resented that child from the moment he was born. Christopher was angelic, you see, and Felicity . . . wasn't. Why do you ask?

I gripped the arm of the chair, torn between rage and relief. "Because Felicity's played an unspeakably cruel joke on her brother. . . ."

With mounting anger, I recounted Lady Havorford's accusations and the devastating effect they'd had on Kit. As I described his journey of atonement, the souls he'd prayed for and the people he'd helped along the way, I began to feel a certain sense of pity for the woman whose lies had sent him on his pilgrimage. Felicity Havorford had all the wealth in the world and Kit had nothing, but I knew who was the richer of the two.

Dimity was less forgiving than I. *I imagine Felicity bridled when you mentioned Christopher's donation to the soup kitchen in Stepney.*

"She said he wasted his inheritance on undeserving strangers," I told her.

There you are, then. She hates Christopher for letting the money go out of the family, not for murdering his father. I imagine that was her aim all along—playing upon his guilt in order to coerce him into transmitting his inheritance to her son.

"But she's already wealthy," I pointed out, giving the devil her due.

In debt up to her eyeteeth, I shouldn't wonder. She always was. Don't waste your pity on Felicity Havorford, Lori. It was monstrous of her to tell such wicked lies and naïve of Christopher to believe them. A few heated words from an overwrought teenager didn't drive Sir Miles mad. The war did.

"I suspected as much," I said.

Your instincts served you well. Sir Miles Anscombe was a casualty of war just as surely as if his plane had been shot down. His wounds were invisible, but fatal nonetheless, and he sustained them long before Christopher was born. And now Felicity has compounded her wickedness by abandoning her brother in his hour of need.

"Don't worry about Kit," I said. "Julian and I will take care of him. We both owe Kit an awful lot. He saved Julian's life, and . . ." I looked into the fire and saw once more the candles burning in Saint Joseph's Church. "He helped me, too."

In what way?

"He forced me to look at things I didn't want to see," I said, "and remember things I wanted to forget. If Kit hadn't come to the cottage, I wouldn't have gone to Saint Benedict's. And if I hadn't gone to Saint Benedict's, I wouldn't have realized how much I have in common with the men there."

He reminded you of the difficult times you've been through. Not everyone would welcome such a reminder.

"I fought it tooth and nail." I let my gaze travel around the room, from the exquisite antique ornaments dangling from the mantel's garland to the fine old oak desk standing before the ivy-webbed window. "I'd gotten too fat and sassy, Dimity. I'd paid my dues, so I thought I was entitled to my blessings. Kit reminded me that blessings aren't a right—they're a gift. I'm no more entitled to them than the men at Saint Benedict's, and I'm ashamed of myself for not remembering it sooner."

Shame can be a useful tool, if it inspires you to share your blessings. You have the Westwood Trust at your command, Lori. You can use it to heal many wounds.

"I will," I assured her, "but it's not enough for me right now to help people from a distance. I'm going back to Saint Benedict's to work, and I'm bringing the boys with me. I don't want Rob and Will growing up in a cocoon. They'll head the Westwood Trust one day. They have to know, from the inside, why it's so important."

So finding a tramp in your drive wasn't such a dreadful nuisance after all.

"It was a blessing in one heck of a disguise." I smiled briefly, then let my thoughts drift back to Kit. "Kit must have finished his pilgrimage," I said. "That's why he tried to burn the scroll. But why did he come here? Why did he choose to end his journey at the cottage?"

For a moment, the page remained blank. Then the handwriting began to curl slowly across the page, as if Dimity were drawing on memories so distant that it took time for her to piece the words together.

Christopher was ten years old when Miles Anscombe sold Anscombe Manor. A few days before the family left for London, Christopher rode over to visit me. He told me he was terrified of living in the city, but he made me promise not to tell his father. Sir Miles wasn't afraid of anything, he said. Sir Miles would be ashamed to learn that his son was such a coward.

Christopher brought along a wooden box, filled with his father's medals. He showed them to me, as if offering proof of his father's bravery, and he told me that whenever he felt frightened,

he would look at the medals and remind himself that he was a
hero's son. As he turned to go, he promised to come back one
day, when he'd grown into the kind of man his father could be
proud of.

I think Christopher was simply keeping his promise.

The fire snapped and hissed, and the wind moaned in
the chimney. There are many kinds of bravery, I mused,
and many battlefields. If medals were awarded for compassion, Kit would be as highly decorated as his father.

There was a knock at the study door. I barely had time
to close the journal before Bill strode in and stood before
me, tapping his foot.

"Time's up," he declared.

I put the journal on the ottoman, wedged snugly between Reginald and Lancaster, and allowed myself to be
pulled to my feet and hustled down the hallway.

"What's the hurry?" I demanded, as he pushed me out
of the front door.

"You'll find out," he replied.

The blinking lights had, mercifully, been doused. A velvet breeze caressed my face and the waxing moon sailed
through ragged clouds, silvering the cottage and throwing
aquamarine shadows across the snow.

"Bill—" I began.

"Hush," he said. "Listen."

I held my breath and heard, faintly, through the crisp
night air, Saint George's bells ringing a joyous peal. We
stood for a moment in silence, listening to the midnight
bells; then Bill put his arms around me.

"I'm sorry about the way things worked out this year,"
he said. "If I recall correctly, you and I were supposed to
spend the past two weeks curled up in front of the hearth,
surrounded by our family."

"Our family's grown a lot since you've been away," I told

him. "It stretches beyond the cottage, beyond the village, to a world of people we haven't even met."

"It sounds as if we'll need a bigger hearth next year," said Bill.

"Do you mind?" I asked.

"How can I object to anything that makes your eyes shine so brightly?" He tilted my chin up. "Still, you have to admit, this Christmas didn't go exactly as planned."

I thought of Kit and Julian, of Saint Benedict's and Saint Joseph's, of the poor, the sick, the hungry, the insane, and I thought of all the blessings I could share, all the candles I could light to keep the darkness of despair at bay.

"It went as planned," I said, "by someone showing me a better way to celebrate his Son's birthday." Rejoicing, I lifted my face to the stars and whispered, "Merry Christmas."

Epilogue

Kit woke up three days after Christmas. Dr. Pritchard telephoned the following morning to tell me that his patient was alert and much stronger than expected, as if, as Matron had predicted, his body had simply needed a good, long rest to recover from its many deprivations.

I drove to Oxford in the canary-yellow Range Rover Bill had presented to me on Christmas morning. My beloved Morris Mini would serve for local jaunts, he'd reasoned, but regular trips to Saint Benedict's called for something more reliable. I was so pleased with my new toy that I kept smiling even after he told me that he'd chosen the eye-popping color "to give other drivers fair warning" of my presence on the road.

I brought with me the funds raised by the Nativity play, boxes of food collected by the villagers, and most of the toys Bill and I had purchased for the twins. The food and funds would go to Saint Benedict's, but the toys would find a home in the children's wards at the Radcliffe. Will and

Rob, who'd spent their first Christmas playing happily with empty boxes and wrapping paper, would never miss them.

Kit had been disconnected from the bank of monitors and moved from the glass-walled cubicle to a private room, but Nurse Willoughby was still in attendance. When I asked after Julian, she told me that he'd missed his morning rounds two days in a row, owing to a massive plumbing failure at Saint Benedict's. She looked at me askance when the distressing news brought a smile to my face, and left me at the door to Kit's room with the usual admonitions about overtiring our patient.

Kit was dozing when I entered. His hospital bed had been cranked into its upright position, and the lamp on the bedside table had been left on. The room was pleasant but anonymous. I saw no sign of Christmas anywhere, save for the brightly wrapped gifts the villagers had sent, which lay unopened on the windowsill.

Kit's close-cropped hair had grown out enough to need combing since I'd last seen him, but he was still clean-shaven. The windburned patches on his face had healed, and his collarbones no longer protruded so sharply beneath the pale-blue hospital gown. His hands, lying peacefully atop the coverlet, were miraculously unblemished by frostbite. I hung my coat on the back of the door, set the canvas carryall on the bedside table, and stood gazing at his hands, remembering the first time I'd seen them, splayed in the snow beneath my lilac bushes.

"You've been here before," said a voice. It was low and musical, every bit as magical as Anne Somerville and Father Danos had remembered it.

"Yes." I gazed into the violet eyes I'd first seen scarcely ten days ago and felt as if I'd known them all of my life. "I'm Lori. Lori Shepherd."

"My good angel," said Kit. "Nurse Willoughby's told me about you."

"Nurse Willoughby's prone to exaggeration," I warned. "I've got a long way to go before I earn my wings."

"Nurse Willoughby also told me that Dimity Westwood is dead."

"I'm sorry," I said. "She died at about the same time you started your journey. I don't suppose you spent much time scanning obits while you were on the road."

"I had other, more practical uses for newspaper." Kit's eyes twinkled briefly, then clouded over. "I still can't believe she's gone. I somehow thought she'd go on forever, like the Pyms."

"Why did you need to see her so badly?" I asked. "I mean, the weather was so awful and you were so sick . . ."

"I was too ill to know how ill I was." Kit smoothed the edge of the coverlet with his fingers. "But Dimity was always a part of the plan. Once I'd finished my journey, I wasn't sure what to do next. I hoped Dimity would tell me."

"You came to her for advice," I said.

"And to thank her. She helped me once before, you see." His restless hands became still. "When my mother died, Dimity told me that grief could be a teacher. It could make me more aware of other people's pain and better able to ease it. I was too young to understand her then, but years later her words came back to me. They were like a beacon, lighting the way through the darkest days of my life. If it hadn't been for Dimity, grief might have overwhelmed me. Instead, it became my ally, helping me to help others." Kit's lips quirked upward in a small, ironic smile. "I even brought a gift for her, to thank her for her guidance."

I took the suede pouch from the carryall and passed it to

him, saying, "This was in your coat pocket when my husband and I found you."

Kit opened the pouch, but instead of spilling the contents onto the coverlet, he fished out a single item and placed it in my palm. "It's a Pathfinder badge," he said softly. "I wanted Dimity to have it. I wish I could have told her how much her words meant to me."

I closed my hand over the slender golden eagle. "I'm sure she's still listening."

"You may be right." Kit drew the pouch's drawstrings tight and returned it to the carryall. "You'll think it daft, but for the past few days I've had the strongest sense of her presence." He grimaced ruefully. "She's been scolding me, telling me to stop worrying my friends and wake up."

"I'm glad she got through to you," I said, smiling inwardly, "because I have a couple of job offers to pass along." I told him of Mr. Barlow's offer of employment and of a brand-new scheme I'd worked out with the Harrises. "Emma and Derek will need someone to run the stable, come spring," I concluded. "And Derek'll have an apartment fitted out by then, overlooking the stable yard and the old orchard. The job's yours, if you want it."

"There's no place I'd rather be than Anscombe Manor." Kit lowered his dark lashes. "But I no longer have the right to live there."

"Yes," I said, "you do." I took the blue journal from my shoulder bag and placed it in his hands. "I've brought a . . . a message for you, from Dimity. I'll wait outside while you read it."

I left the room quickly, before he could ask any questions, and stood in the corridor, just outside his door, wondering if I'd been right to entrust him with the secret of the blue journal. I wasn't worried about him betraying my trust so much as having a relapse when Aunt Dimity's handwriting appeared. The blue journal had given me a turn when I'd first seen it in action, and I'd been in tip-top health at the time.

Still, I reminded myself, drastic situations called for drastic measures, and only Dimity could provide Kit with the answers he so desperately needed.

"Lori!" Julian's shout cut through the background noise in the bustling corridor as he took the long hallway at a run. When he slid to a stop in front of me, he was out of breath and flushed with exertion, as though he'd jogged all the way from Saint Benedict's. "I'd've been here sooner, but I've been up to my elbows in . . . well, never mind. How's Kit?" he asked, looking eagerly at the door.

"He's fine, but he needs to be alone for a while," I cautioned. "I've brought him some new information about his father. He needs time to digest it."

"What new information?" Julian asked.

I took a deep breath. "The good news is that Kit wasn't responsible for his father's death. The bad news is that Sir Miles was more deeply disturbed than Kit realized."

"Few blessings are unmixed," Julian observed. "Who told you about Sir Miles?"

"I read something Dimity Westwood wrote about him," I replied, telling the exact truth and no more. "And given a choice between Lady Havorford's version of the truth and Dimity's, I'll take Dimity's every time."

Julian sighed. "Lady Havorford is a troubled soul. Hatred is poisoning her spirit."

"She's trouble, all right," I said. "But she won't bother Kit anymore. He's got a new family now, and we'll stand by him."

"Amen." Julian stood back to examine me. "You're

looking remarkable cheerful, Lori. Was Father Christmas kind to you?"

I colored to my roots as I remembered just how kind Father Christmas had been once I'd dragged him off to bed on Christmas Eve.

"If I'm cheerful, it's because I've come up with a killer fund-raising scheme for Saint Benedict's," I said, hastily redirecting the conversation.

Julian grinned. "Do tell."

"It's your idea, really." I reached into my shoulder bag and handed him a slip of paper. "It's my father's recipe for angel cookies. You told me that I could make a fortune selling them, so I thought, why not use them to raise money for the hostel? Get it?" I held my hands in the air, framing an imaginary slogan. "Be an angel, support Saint Benedict's."

"It's a lovely thought, Lori," said Julian, "but we'd have to bake an awful lot of cookies to raise the kind of money Saint Benedict's needs. We simply can't afford the ingredients."

"Not to worry," I said. "I've already arranged for Shuttleworth Bakeries to make and distribute the cookies. They'll sell them all over the country and donate seventy percent of the proceeds to Saint Benedict's."

"S-seventy percent?" Julian said wonderingly. "You drive a hard bargain."

"I'm a powder puff," I confessed. "It's my father-in-law who drives a hard bargain. But wait, there's more." I dipped into my shoulder bag again and waved an oversized manila envelope under Julian's nose.

"Another recipe?" he guessed.

"Nope." I felt a shivery thrill of anticipation as I announced, "Julian, it is my pleasure to present you with the title to the new Saint Benedict's."

"I . . . I beg your pardon?" he said, blinking rapidly.

"My friend Derek Harris took a look at the old Saint Benedict's while you and I were in London and he says it'll take at least a year to renovate," I explained. "It'd be ridiculous to have the men sleep in the streets for a whole year, so I bought a new building instead. I've cleared it with the bishop, and Derek's ready to outfit the new place to your specifications."

"It's a magnificent gesture, Lori," Julian said, frowning worriedly, "but are you sure you can afford it?"

I laughed out loud. "I guess I never mentioned that I'm the head of the Westwood Trust. Apart from that, I've got about a bazillion dollars of my own lying around, collecting interest. It's time I put a chunk of it to good use." I tapped the envelope excitedly. "The new building's about six blocks from where you are now—four stories, blond brick, with a fenced parking area—"

"I know the place." Julian put a hand to his forehead. "I prayed that it would somehow come to us one day, but I never imagined . . ."

I clucked my tongue in disapproval. "Isn't there something about faith in your job description?"

"Lori," he said huskily, "I—I don't know how to thank you."

"You've got it backwards, Julian. This is my way of thanking you." I took his hand and tucked the envelope into it. "Merry Christmas, Father Bright."

The call light above Kit's doorway winked on and off. I tugged Julian into the room and left him standing near the door, staring dazedly at the manila envelope. As I approached the bed I saw the canvas carryall lying open on the bedside table and Lancaster nestled in the crook of Kit's arm. The blue journal lay beneath Kit's folded hands.

He was slightly flushed, but composed, and his violet eyes never left my face.

"Will you take the job at Anscombe Manor?" I asked.

Kit nodded slowly. "As soon as I'm strong enough."

"What job is that?" Julian asked, emerging from his trance, but before Kit or I could answer, he exclaimed, "Good heavens, what's happened to Lancaster?"

The little brown horse was no longer the patched and faded toy Kit had left behind at Blackthorne Farm. His brown cotton hide was smooth and spotless, his mane and tail were complete and neatly combed, and his black button eyes twinkled in the lamplight.

Julian came to stand beside me. "Did you restore him, Lori?"

Kit's eyes danced as I struggled to find an answer that was both truthful and accurate, but he gallantly came to my rescue.

"Let's just say," he murmured, gazing down at the blue journal, "that Lancaster's stay at the cottage did him a world of good."

Julian nodded absently, too caught up in his own euphoria to worry over niggling details. He spied the wrapped packages on the windowsill and declared, "It looks as though a belated Christmas is in order. Shall we?"

"By all means," said Kit.

We sampled Sally Pyne's hand-dipped chocolates, stacked Mr. Wetherhead's magazines on the bedside table, and draped the warm winter clothing from Kitchen's Emporium across Kit's bed. Finally, Julian scrounged three drinking glasses from a supply cabinet down the hall and poured a tot of the Peacocks' homemade brandy into each.

"A toast." He raised his glass. "To blessings shared."

"To answered prayers," Kit chimed in.

I looked from Kit to Julian to the blue journal, lying buried beneath a scattering of bright ribbons, and thought of my father, opening his heart and hand to heal a wounded world. I hoped that he was listening as I raised my glass and said, "To a truly perfect Christmas."

Angel Cookies

1 cup softened butter
1 cup sugar
2 large eggs, lightly beaten

2 teaspoons vanilla
3½ cups all-purpose flour
1 teaspoon baking powder

In a bowl, cream butter and sugar. Add the eggs and the vanilla. Mix until combined well.

In a bowl, sift flour and baking powder together.

Add the dry ingredients to the butter mixture and beat until mixture forms a dough. If easy to handle, roll out immediately; if sticky, wrap in plastic and chill for two hours or overnight.

Preheat oven to 350°F.

Divide dough in half. On a lightly floured surface, roll out half the dough into a ¼-inch-thick round. Cut out angel shapes and arrange 1 inch apart on lightly greased baking sheets. Repeat for remaining dough.

Bake for 8 to 10 minutes or until lightly golden around the edges.

Transfer to racks to cool. Frost with Confectioners' Frosting.

Yield: about 2 dozen cookies.

Confectioners' Frosting

⅓ cup softened butter
⅛ teaspoon salt

2 cups confectioners' sugar
2 tablespoons cream

Cream the butter and the salt together, then beat in the sugar. Stir in the cream and beat well, adding more sugar or more cream as needed to get the proper consistency.